"I want to marry you,"

Gabe said.

"Why?" Blair pressed him for an answer, knowing he wouldn't have one. Gabriel Sloan had never wanted any encumbrances in his solitary life. Things couldn't have changed that much.

"Because he's my son, and I owe it to him," he exploded. "And because you're his mother and I owe you, too. I should never have..."

So he felt guilty for that one night of indiscretion? Blair smiled bitterly. Well, it was as good a reason as any to suggest marriage, she supposed. It just wasn't her reason, not the one she'd dreamed of, anyway.

He might be willing to marry her, but in the end she would turn him down cold. Daniel was *her* son, and she intended him to feel the love in his life. Gabe didn't believe in love.

And Blair couldn't settle for anything else.

Books by Lois Richer

Love Inspired

A Will and a Wedding #8
†*Faithfully Yours* #15
†*A Hopeful Heart* #23
†*Sweet Charity* #32
A Home, a Heart, a Husband #50
This Child of Mine #59
Baby on the Way #73
Daddy on the Way #79
Wedding on the Way #85
‡*Mother's Day Miracle* #101
‡*His Answered Prayer* #115

†Faith, Hope & Charity
*Brides of the Seasons
‡If Wishes Were Weddings

LOIS RICHER

lives in a small Canadian prairie town with her husband, who, she says, is a "wanna-be farmer." She began writing in self-defense, as a way to escape. She says, "Come spring, tomato plants take over my flower beds, no matter how many I 'accidentally' pull up or 'prune.' By summer I'm fielding phone calls from neighbors who don't need tomatoes this fall. Come September, no one visits us, and anyone who gallantly offers to take a box invariably ends up with six. I have more recipes with tomatoes than with chocolate. Thank goodness for writing! Imaginary people with imaginary gardens are much easier to deal with!"

Lois is pleased to present this latest book in her new series IF WISHES WERE WEDDINGS for the Steeple Hill Love Inspired line. Please feel free to contact Lois at: Box 639, Nipawin, Saskatchewan, S0E 1E0, Canada.

His Answered Prayer

Lois Richer

Love Inspired®

Published by Steeple Hill Books™

If you purchased this book without a cover you should be aware
that this book is stolen property. It was reported as "unsold and
destroyed" to the publisher, and neither the author nor the
publisher has received any payment for this "stripped book."

STEEPLE HILL BOOKS

Steeple Hill™

ISBN 0-373-87121-X

HIS ANSWERED PRAYER

Copyright © 2000 by Lois Richer

All rights reserved. Except for use in any review, the reproduction
or utilization of this work in whole or in part in any form by any
electronic, mechanical or other means, now known or hereafter
invented, including xerography, photocopying and recording, or in
any information storage or retrieval system, is forbidden without
the written permission of the editorial office, Steeple Hill Books,
300 East 42nd Street, New York, NY 10017 U.S.A.

All characters in this book have no existence outside the imagination of
the author and have no relation whatsoever to anyone bearing the same
name or names. They are not even distantly inspired by any individual
known or unknown to the author, and all incidents are pure invention.

This edition published by arrangement with Steeple Hill Books.

® and TM are trademarks of Steeple Hill Books, used under license.
Trademarks indicated with ® are registered in the United States Patent
and Trademark Office, the Canadian Trade Marks Office and in other
countries.

Visit us at www.steeplehill.com

Printed in U.S.A.

This is my commandment, that you love one
another, as I have loved you.

—*John* 15:12

This book is for kids everywhere, big or little, who hurt because Mommy or Daddy isn't there. Your Father above is waiting with open arms.

Chapter One

"Mommy?"

"Yes, Daniel."

"Where is my daddy?"

"Uh…"

"I'm gonna pray really hard, so God will send me a daddy."

Blair Delaney sighed, her son's earnest question from last night still ringing in her ears. Daniel hadn't waited for the answer she didn't have—or at least, one he'd understand—but had bluntly petitioned heaven with his heartfelt demand.

She shoved her hair behind her ear and deliberately pushed the problem of Daniel's absent father out of her mind. It was procrastination of the worst sort, but she couldn't deal with it now. She had to focus on the tasks at hand. Her family depended on her. They needed her to be strong, to keep things on track, to take care of them.

She picked up the shortwave radio and pressed the button.

"I'm heading for the hives in the west field, Mac. If I'm lucky and things are as good as they seem out here, I won't have to feed the bees sugar for much longer now."

"That's good, Busy Bee."

The old nickname drew a grin. Trust Grandpa to put a smile into her day. She wasn't going to let him down. Somehow she'd manage Daniel and all the other little problems that kept creeping up, demanding her attention.

"It'll be nice for you to stop making these runs every day." Mac's voice came strong and clear, proof positive that he was once more feeling up to snuff.

Blair let out a breath of relief. That lingering winter cold that had rattled around in his chest since December scared her. Maybe it was finally gone. Blair heard him ask how long she'd be.

"The thing is, I'm not sure, Grandpa. Daniel will be at kindergarten till three. I should be back long before the bus gets there. Can you check on Aunt Willie for me, make sure she takes her medication on time?"

Mac's ready answer sent a shaft of pleasure straight to her heart. Sometimes it was nice to be needed, to do things that really mattered to the ones you loved.

Blair snapped the radio into its holder seconds before she had to grab the wheel and force it right on the rutted, muddy road. Spring in the valley made it tough to negotiate the unpaved foothill roads that bordered Colorado's famous Rocky Mountains. But when the valley sprouted this bright vibrant wash of color, she couldn't wish herself anyplace else. This was home.

Ten minutes later Blair surveyed the first blush of

green that tipped the branches surrounding her field. Below her feet, tiny plants forced their way through the soil and stretched to meet the sun. It was fresh, it was good. It was hers.

Or it would be one day.

Blair strode across the meadow where she'd set out her beehives, the same meadow she'd worked so hard to make a profit on. As she walked, her mind focused on Daniel's upcoming field trip. The class kitty was still short of the requisite funds. His teacher needed her to organize one more fund-raiser before the end of May. Blair would have to come up with a plan. Just another little job to see to.

The hives seemed in good repair, once she removed the outer insulating wraps. A quick check inside proved the durability of this particular strain of bees, and she pushed away any lingering doubts she'd had about spending so much on them.

"With any luck at all, this will be a banner year for Mind Your Own Beeswax." The words brought a satisfied smile to her lips.

The company had been her idea over six years ago, just after her life had fallen apart. She'd run home to Grandpa Mac and his sister Wilhelmina. Even though they were barely scraping by on the tumbledown ranch they'd chosen for retirement, they welcomed her, and Daniel when he'd arrived, with open arms. They needed her, and Blair had willingly pitched in. Her fledgling honey and beeswax candle business really took off after Daniel's birth and now consumed most of Blair's time.

With a practiced eye she studied the field. The Merrihews always planted early. That was one of the reasons she chose to rent to them. That and the fact that their clover crops provided exactly the environment her bees needed.

Blair mentally calculated how much her earnings and Mac's pension brought in and then subtracted the costs of Willie's special expenses and the costs involved in helping their friend Albert Hunter. He had a predilection for inventions that never quite took off.

"It's going to be a stretch," she muttered, unwilling to even consider what would happen if her grandfather were no longer there. She didn't love him just for his pension, though he'd teased her about it often enough!

If I could just expand a bit, she thought, turning to survey the hilly terrain beyond. But where?

A movement to the left caught her attention, and she frowned. Someone was out there. Blair walked to the truck, trying to identify the lone figure perched atop a mound of dirt, studying the southern portion of her valley through a surveyor's transom.

"Not another one! Why won't these guys take no for an answer? We're *not* going to sell. This is part of Daniel's heritage." The land wasn't as good as a daddy, of course, but next to love, it was all she had to give her son.

She scrambled around the edge of the field, hiding herself in the bushes and trees that surrounded the area so she'd be able to sneak up behind the intruder. She needn't have bothered. He didn't seem to notice her or anything else around him, lost as he was in his scribbling on the small notebook he'd pulled out of his pants pocket after checking his sighting once more. He was so totally immersed in his own world that the snap of a twig beneath her feet didn't break his concentration.

When she was about fifty feet away, Blair left her cover and moved into the open.

"You're trespassing," she called loudly, hoping to startle the interloper.

He jerked upright, his body tall and lean and still. Then, ever so slowly, he turned around. Blair gasped.

"You!" She clenched her fists against her thighs as all the hurt of the past welled up inside. "What are you doing here, Gabriel?"

Gabe Sloan stood there in his sand-washed silk shirt, designer jeans and Italian leather boots, a twisted smile rolling across his handsome face. His hair, jet-black and poker straight, lay in its familiar style, cut close to the head. Eyes, those piercing mossy green eyes, took in every detail of her appearance.

"Blair," he murmured, his lips barely moving. "The trusting, always truthful, *disappearing* Blair Delaney." His mouth slashed a chilly grin. "To what do I owe the honor of your sudden return to my life?" He stared at her like a hawk sighting a mouse. But his voice exhibited total disinterest in her answer.

"I'm not in your life, Gabe," she whispered, unable to believe what she was seeing, though the sinking in the pit of her stomach assured her he was there. "In fact, I never was. Not the way I wanted to be. You never needed me, remember? You don't need anybody."

His face tightened, and his eyes hardened. His wide mouth pinched in a stiff little smile. He avoided her glare.

"Part of that is true. Though why you had to take off, run away like a scared young rabbit is beyond me." Gabe sighed, his whole body shifting. "It doesn't matter anymore, does it? You were too young—for a lot of things. I should have known that.'' He shook his head, eyes hard but with an underlying rueful glint that flashed to meet hers.

''I had a duty to protect my company, Blair. Whether you liked it or not.''

She tossed her head, angry that he was still using his company as an excuse to push her away. ''Uh-uh. You wanted me to sign that prenuptial agreement to protect *yourself*. It was obvious you had no intention of putting everything into our marriage. You'd already provided a way out!''

He laughed, a short harsh bark that told her he hadn't changed his view of her, or people in general. Gabe always believed someone was out to cheat him. She watched as he turned that suspicion her way.

''You don't understand because you never had a head for business, Blair. You were too deep into your chemistry formulas and theories. So go ahead. Pile all the guilt you want on my head. I've been through it before. You won't say anything somebody hasn't already left at my door. Fortunately, you got away in time, before regrets got the better of you.''

A lot he knew! She regretted so many things. Blair shook her head. She wasn't going back to that misery of self-doubt. She wasn't ever going back. He wouldn't do that to her again.

''The only thing I'm interested in chewing you out for is your presence on my land. I'd like you to leave, Gabe.''

''Your land?'' The great Gabriel Sloan frowned, obviously confused by her protest. ''This is my land. And I have the papers to prove it.''

''Don't be ridiculous!'' Blair snapped, furious that

now, at this stage of the game, he was still looking for an ulterior motive. "We hold the deed to all of this property."

"We?" His body stiffened, eyes alert as he digested this bit of information. "Are you married?"

"It's none of your business." She returned his stare with a glare that usually made people look away. But Gabriel wasn't like other people. "No," she finally admitted.

"But you always said, uh—" he thought a moment "—that your parents were dead." He peered at the ground, frowning, obviously sifting through what little he could remember as he kicked at a clump of dirt.

Blair could almost hear that computerlike brain of his clicking through the file of information he had about her, deleting this byte, updating that one. Finally he spoke.

"The only people you ever talked about were your grandfather and some aunt. I don't remember anything about Colorado."

"That's hardly surprising."

Blair swallowed the rest of her snappy comeback at the impaling glint of those now-emerald eyes. She remembered how those eyes changed color to suit his mood. That intense scrutiny, that ability to look right through her, they all combined to send twitching jitters skipping over her nerves.

"Should I have asked, Blair?"

Blair fumed at the spin he put on her words. She'd forgotten how good he was at twisting what she said. He made it sound as if she'd woven a web of deceit instead of opening her heart up to him, only to have it thrown back in her face!

"I never lied to you, Gabe." At least, only by admission.

"Does that mean you and your family live around here now?" He studied her curiously, his eyes roving slowly over the top of her head to the tumble of lopsided curls she'd raked her hair into this morning on her way to the truck.

Slowly his gaze flowed past the big bulky sweater, ragged jeans and muddy cowboy boots. Then he glanced across the fields that would soon blossom with flowers.

"I never took you for the down-home, country type, Blair."

"You never really knew me." She let the sharp words pour out, angry that Gabe even imagined he'd known the person inside of her. "That much was obvious from the way you used me."

"I didn't use you!" His face washed in a red tide of anger. "It wasn't my fault you expected too much."

"I did, didn't I?" she agreed quietly, turning to stare at the gorgeous blue sky that sparkled over the snowcapped mountains in the distance. She squeezed her eyes shut, forcing down the lump in her throat. "Way too much, as it turns out."

Please help me, she prayed desperately. *I never thought I'd see him again. I thought You would lead me to someone else. I don't want this!*

"Blair? What are you doing? Open your eyes!" His hand on her arm helped wake her to the fact that her reality had changed. The peace she'd always found in this valley was shattered, shifted into something ominous that could turn on her if she wasn't careful.

Blair jerked her arm out of his grasp and whirled away, anxious to put as much distance between them as possible.

"I'm fine. There's nothing for you here, Gabriel Sloan. Nothing! This is my family's land. I'd like you to leave."

He stayed where he was, saying nothing. And when Blair couldn't take his silence for one moment longer, she headed for her truck.

"Blair?"

His softly voiced request made her stop in her tracks.

"It's my land now. At least part of it is. I did buy it. Free and clear. No encumbrances."

She shouldn't be surprised. It was the way he'd always preferred to live—never let anyone get too close. The words pricked a nerve in her mind. Blair whirled, her forehead wrinkled in a frown. He sounded so positive of his right to be here.

"Not possible, Gabriel. You must have the wrong place. This particular quarter section is my grandfather's. He's had it in his family for years. He's willing it to me when he dies."

Gabe seemed unabashed by her assurance. He simply shrugged, then pulled out a piece of paper from his pocket.

As he read the legal description to one of the three quarters Mac owned, Blair felt the bottom tilt out of her world.

"No." She shook her head stubbornly. "Someone has made a mistake."

"Perhaps you?" His mouth tilted in a questioning quirk. Blair took the document and scanned it, her eyes halting abruptly when they fell on the signature at the bottom.

"Mac?" she whispered. "Mac actually sold you this?"

"Mackenzie Rhodes." He nodded. "He wrote to me, offered to sell me a little bit of heaven about four months ago. I had someone check it out, then decided to buy. This is the first time I've seen anything other than the videos and snapshots that were taken." He stopped, one eyebrow quirked upward. "Is it a problem?"

Blair sucked in a deep breath and concentrated. Hard.

"It's a mistake," she mumbled at last. "It has to be. He wouldn't do this to me. He wouldn't. Not Mac." It was the only solution she could some up with. "Not my own grandfather," Blair asserted, giving a vigorous shake to her head. "He knows how much I depend on this land."

"You do?" Gabe surveyed the area with interest. "Why does a chemist with your qualifications depend on this particular land? And for what?"

Her *qualifications?* If he only knew.

"I need it for my business." She saw the jerk of his head and compressed her lips tightly, stemming the diatribe that ached for release. "I have to earn my way, you know."

"Don't we all." There it was again, that sardonic twist that manipulated his attractive mouth into a mocking sneer. "Are you doing a field study or something?"

"I have hives all around this field." At his skeptical look she lifted a hand and pointed. "There, see those white boxes? And there?"

Gabe squinted into the distance, then finally nodded.

"That's only a small number of the hives that provide the honey I sell. I also make candles, though I doubt you've heard of my company." She told him the name and shrugged when his eyes didn't light up. "I didn't think so. We're pretty new on the scene." She shifted uncomfortably. "What are you staring at?"

"You. I can't seem to see you sticky with honey." His smile begged her to see the joke. "You always looked so elegant, so refined. If Eunice Standish could see her model for women's fashions now, what would she think?"

Anger snipped at Blair. How dare he malign her for making an honest living? How would somebody as rich and spoiled as Gabe ever understand how hard it was to provide just the daily bread for four other people?

"I only took that part-time job because it paid so well. And to please you, so I'd look the way you wanted." She shrugged carelessly. "Now I don't really care what you or Eunice or anyone else thinks. This is *my* life." She straightened to her full height and frowned. "As interesting as this is, Gabe, I do have work to do. I'd appreciate it if you'd leave now."

"What *work* do you have to do today?"

She jerked her head at his curious tone, but could find nothing derogatory in his eyes. Maybe she's misjudged him. Maybe he had changed. She shrugged and grudgingly told him.

"I'm going to unwrap the last of the hives. I've done most of the ones on the south side, but I left a few hives in this field till today because that part of the hill takes longer to thaw out.''

"Can I watch?"

Blair sighed. Why now? Why here? Why today? Couldn't he have gone hunting for land somewhere else? Why did he want land, anyway? The Gabriel Sloan she knew scorned any place that didn't boast all the amenities of his deluxe L.A. condo.

"Blair? I promise I won't interfere."

"If you do you'll get stung!" That made her smile. She wondered if he'd understand her hidden meaning.

"It's happened before. A certain college student used to do it quite often, as it happens. I missed her."

Blair got caught up in the storm of sea foam that swirled in his eyes. Her breath caught, reminding her how easily Gabe Sloan could draw her in, make her believe she was the most precious thing in his life. It wouldn't happen again.

"I doubt you even noticed I was gone," she returned sourly. "I'm sure you were too involved in the latest gizmo and high-tech security to keep it under wraps." She wished it wasn't true, but reality was hard to ignore.

"I noticed, Blair. Especially when I had to cancel that elaborate wedding." His voice growled low, full of mocking innuendo. "Caterers, church, flowers, it took a lot of time."

And money. Blair heard the words even if he didn't say them. She forced her foot not to stamp. He was thinking about the money again, she just knew it. The one thing that had managed to uproot a love she was sure they'd share until eternity.

Gabe studied her, head tilted to one side in that

familiar pose, and Blair smiled at the gesture so exactly a mirror of Daniel's.

Daniel!

"I—that is, I have to get busy. You can trail along if you want. Or not. I don't care." She stalked through the bushes, ignoring the whoosh of mud as her boots found firm passage through the spring runoff.

She could hear Gabe following her but ignored him.

It didn't take long to get to the last few hives and undo their insulated covers. She folded them carefully, then turned to face him.

"That's all there is to the show for today, Gabe. I've got to get home and get to work. There's a lot to do. Goodbye."

He said nothing, simply stood there, studying her as if she were one of the oddly hewn pieces of smooth alabaster he'd collected so avidly six years ago.

"Can you find your way out of here?"

She tossed the hive wrappers into the back of the truck then turned to face him, hands clamped to her hips.

"Blair, I have legal title to this land, and I'm not backing out. This is exactly the kind of place I've been looking for." His lips clamped shut, the expression on his face changed, hardened. "Perhaps the best thing to do is check it out. Now. Before things go much further."

"What things?" She gaped at him, her mind numb.

"An excavation crew is set to come in here Monday morning."

"Excavation?" Blair blanched at the thought of her beautiful valley, destroyed. "Why?"

"I'm building a house. I intend to live in this valley, Blair. It's going to be my home."

She couldn't take it in, couldn't understand what kind of a joke he was playing.

"But you live in Los Angeles," she reminded him, depicting the picture she remembered late at night when she should have slept. "You crave bright lights, fast cars and people you can impress by ignoring them." Yes, that was the real Gabe. "Why would you move *here,* to the middle of nowhere?"

It didn't make sense. None of this did. Gabriel Sloan was as city as they came. Going out with starlets, winning at squash, traveling on the big showy jet, those were the things he needed to prove himself. Gabe craved all the glitz and glamour of the nightlife that L.A. offered. There was nothing around here that would interest him.

His voice roused her from her introspection.

"I'm experimenting, Blair. Isn't that what you used to encourage? I want something different from my life. The company just isn't enough anymore. It bores me. I've hired a manager. I want to take some time and relax for a while. Consider what's next."

"You've let go of the reins?" She squeaked in disbelief. "You? The guy who thinks everybody's out to take him?" It was a direct quote. He'd said it over six years ago on that fateful morning when all her dreams had died.

Oh, God, where are you? Does he know about Daniel? Is that why he's here?

The very thought made her head spin, and all the blood rushed to her feet. He was going to steal Daniel! And he had money and power enough to do it.

"Blair? Sit down." He pushed her onto a huge

granite slab of glacial rock whose quartz sparkles flashed in the bright sun. His hands rubbed hers, his surprisingly warm and gentle. "You're still as thin as a reed," he muttered, pausing to brush a ringleted tendril from her cheek. "And this hair is still a riot of curls. I didn't think it was possible, but you're thinner. Are you still so busy taking care of everyone else, you don't take care of yourself?"

She pulled away, but she had no energy to get up. Not yet.

"I'm fine. I'm just busy. I guess I forgot to eat breakfast." As if that would have changed anything. She glared at him. "Why now, Gabe? Why here?"

"I wanted a change. And I was intrigued by his description. Heaven on earth. Who wouldn't want that?"

There was a bitter tilt to his lips that made her wonder if Gabe had suffered some financial setbacks she didn't know about. Or perhaps he'd lost the edge that put his company out in front.

"Who indeed?" She was going to strangle Mac when she got hold of him. How could he have sold this land out from under her, especially to Gabe? How could he have set this all up when he knew the risks? And it was a setup. She had no doubts about that.

Gabe picked up her hand. "You've got calluses here," he murmured as his thumb brushed across her palm. "You shouldn't work so hard, Blair."

Yeah, right! Like how else would she live? Blair shifted away from him and clambered awkwardly to her feet. Why was she always so ungraceful whenever he was around? Why did he make her so nervous?

Because of Daniel.

But she hadn't had Daniel to think about back then.

In the old days just the sound of Gabe's voice had made her skin prickle with anticipation.

She shoved the memories away.

"I'm going home to talk to my grandfather," she murmured. "Something isn't right here."

"I assure you it's all perfectly legal. I don't do business any other way." He sounded angry that she'd suspect him of subterfuge. "You should at least remember that much."

Blair didn't respond. Instead, she walked to her truck and climbed in, mulling the whole thing over inside her tired brain.

"No, I know. It's just that Mac said—" She glanced at him, vaguely surprised that he'd followed her. "Never mind. I'll sort it out. You'll probably get a letter canceling the whole deal."

Gabe shook his head and shoved her door closed.

"No, the deal's already been finalized. I'm not allowing anyone to back out now. If you wait a minute, I'll get my vehicle and follow you. I'd like to know the answer to a few questions of my own."

Blair glanced at her watch, then nodded grimly. Daniel wasn't due home for at least another hour. If she hurried, she could get this all sorted out and have Gabe on his way before kindergarten was dismissed for the afternoon.

Twenty minutes later they pulled up in front of her grandfather's old house. She couldn't help contrasting its ramshackle appearance with the elegant, glossy glass-and-chrome condo Gabe had lived in seven years ago. Her battered brown half-ton sat rusting on the spot while his polished black and silver sport utility screamed money. Night and day.

Still, what did it matter? He'd always known that

she wasn't in his league, didn't have money to burn. Her part-time job had been a good one, and she'd been comfortable sharing digs with Clarissa Feather-hawk and Briony Green. But every extra cent she hadn't needed for college went home to Mac and Willie, to repay them.

"Having second thoughts about introducing me to your family?" The mocking query brought her to the present.

Without a word Blair tripped up the stairs to the back door. She opened it, then moved back to allow Gabe in. He stepped out of his expensive boots first, then through the doorway and into the kitchen, his eyes curiously appraising the old farmhouse.

"Mac? Can you come in here? Now?"

Blair stepped out of her boots and grabbed the cof-feepot. Without wasting any movements, she poured two mugs of the steaming black brew, set them on the table and motioned Gabe to sit down.

Gabe raised his eyebrows at her silent order, but took his seat without speaking. He took one sip of the coffee, coughed, then added a generous measure of cream and sugar.

Blair sat and pretended to ignore him.

"Hey, Busy Bee. You're early. How were the hives?" Mac strolled through the hallway and into the kitchen, his eyes widening as he caught sight of Gabe. "Hello."

"Mac, this is Gabriel Sloan. He thinks he's bought the south quarter from you. Gabe, this is my grand-father. The infamous Mackenzie Rhodes of your letter."

Her grandfather flicked an eyebrow at her acid tone, then turned his attention to their guest.

The two men silently sized up each other, shook hands and then sat. Blair glanced from one to the other.

"Well?" she demanded of her grandfather. "Aren't you going to tell him that it's a mistake?"

Mac smiled tenderly and reached out to fold her hand in his.

"No," he murmured. "I'm not. I sold Mr. Sloan the land. It was mine, I had a right to and I did it." His face showed no sign of repentance.

"But, Grandfather, you know that I depend on that land!" Blair felt the sting of his betrayal to the soles of her feet. "How could you sell it to *him?* Why not to me? I would have bought you out!"

She glared at Gabe, who kept his head bent, studying his coffee as if it would metamorphose into his favorite mocha latte. Blair switched her focus to her grandfather.

"Why?"

"You know why," he returned evenly, his face stern. "We've discussed it before. I think it's the right thing to do. It's time. You know that."

Blair pursed her lips, mindful of the heated arguments she'd had with him for months now. Mac believed she owed it to Gabe to tell Daniel's father he had a son. She thought she'd made him understand how foolish it would be to expect Gabe to accept the boy, to believe Gabe could father his child the way Mac had fathered her.

Apparently none of her protests had touched him.

"How can you do this to us?" she said under her breath. "This is my business. You have no right to interfere in my private life."

Mac didn't back down, his dark eyes glossy with

unshed tears. "I have the right of a man who loves his granddaughter more than life." He reached out to pat her cheek. "I'm not young anymore, Busy Bee. I won't be around forever. I want to know my family is okay."

"And this is how you do it? By going against me, behind my back, selling this land out from under me? I can manage for all of us. Haven't I done fine so far?"

A thin high-pitched voice wobbled out a few notes from a well-known hymn. The sound grew louder as Willie entered the kitchen.

"Ooh, what a handsome fellow!" Willie's cooing voice spoke behind Blair's right ear.

Blair sighed. *Not now,* she prayed. *Please don't let Willie blurt out the truth.* "He's yours, isn't he, Blair."

"He's—"

"Mac sold him some land, Willie." Blair broke in, desperate to keep her grandfather from spilling the beans. "The south quarter."

"You *sold* our heritage, Mackenzie?" Willie coughed delicately into her lavender lace handkerchief as she fluttered around the kitchen. "Have things become so bad that we must sell off our birthright to live?"

Blair was about to set her straight, to add further explanations, when she heard a noise outside. Her grandfather sat up straight, her aunt collapsed into a chair and Gabe frowned at them all. Blair couldn't move a muscle as her son came bounding through the door.

"Hi, Mom! The bus came early 'cause the school had a fire." Daniel let his jacket, backpack and lunch bag fall where they would, his gaze fastened on the tall, dark-haired stranger who sat staring at him.

"Hey, you an' me got the same hair," Daniel declared, his mouth stretched wide in a smile. "My mom has a picture of you. Are you the answer?"

Blair gulped down a sob, unable to say a word, though her hands closed over her son's shoulders as she hugged him close for one brief moment, prolonging what she somehow knew would change irrevocably from this moment on.

"The answer?" Gabe swallowed, his eyes swinging from Mac to Blair to the little boy. "I don't know what you mean."

Daniel wiggled himself free of his mother's hold and went to stand in front of the big man. Two pairs of eyes, the same startling green, inspected each other.

"The answer," Daniel explained, "to my prayer. For a daddy. I'm almost six an' I really need a daddy. Are you gonna be him?"

Chapter Two

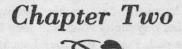

"Gabe, this is my son, Daniel. Daniel, I'd like you to meet Gabriel Sloan."

Gabe almost laughed at the words. She didn't *want* the boy to meet him at all. And he knew why. This child was his son!

Gabe stared at the mirror image of himself at five. The little boy in front of him solemnly shook his hand as the truth smacked Gabe squarely between the eyes. He had a child. He was a father!

"So I was wondering, Mr. Gabriel, are you the one?"

Gabe jerked back to reality with stunned surprise as a small hand carefully patted his arm.

"The one?" he repeated blankly. His eyes sought Blair and he swallowed hard at the pain and worry he found swirling in the depths of her molten chocolate eyes. He focused on the boy. "Uh, I'm not exactly sure just yet."

"Oh." Daniel's mobile face fell with disappointment, but brightened a moment later. "That doesn't mean no," he insisted. "My mom says she's not sure lots of times. It means maybe."

"Right." Gabe swallowed, the thought of parenthood engulfing him in a wash of anxiety. *Not yet,* his brain screamed. *I'm not ready for that yet, God! I've only just taken the first steps to changing my life.*

"It's okay. You can think about it if you want." Daniel smiled, then leaned near Gabe's ear. "But could you hurry up? My teacher says we're having parent-teacher day pretty soon, and Joey Lancaster is bringing his dad. I don't like Joey Lancaster."

Gabe got the implied message loud and clear. *My dad is better than yours.* Poor little tyke! Belatedly he wondered how long Daniel had been praying for a father.

A wave of anger washed over him as he considered how much he'd missed. A baby, a toddler, hugs, good-night kisses, Christmases and birthdays. He'd known none of that. But Blair had. And she'd kept him in the dark. On purpose. That hurt more than he'd ever imagined, though Gabe didn't understand why. He knew he wasn't daddy material. He was a loner. He didn't need anyone. He couldn't afford to.

But she could have told him.

Gabe turned to stare at Blair and immediately rethought his position. He had no rights when it came to Daniel. None. He'd lost them all when Blair, sweet, innocent Blair, walked out of his life with her childish dreams ruined. By him.

"You need me, Gabe," she'd sobbed that morning.

He cringed, remembering his furious response. "I don't need anybody."

"I thought you loved me enough to believe I'm not like the others. I've tried so hard to be what you want, but you still can't see the real me. You can't see beyond the security of your business and your money. You can't see love.''

That memory could still make him ache for her shattered innocence. Blair, backing away from him, hair tumbling around her shoulders in that glossy riot of curls that he'd touched only moments before.

Once, just that once he'd let himself desire something more than security. Daniel was the result. The knowledge ate at him like acid on an open wound.

He'd sent her away with his child.

"You'd better do your chores, Daniel. Maybe Albert will help you." Blair's soft voice broke through his reverie.

Gabe looked up. Who was Albert? Someone Blair was interested in? Was that why Daniel needed a father, to ward off the unwanted attentions of this Albert person?

"Okay." Daniel grabbed two cookies from the nutcracker cookie jar that perched on a low shelf. He whirled to grin at Gabe. "See you later," he offered.

"Yes, you will," Gabe returned evenly, refusing to look at Blair. "I'm glad I met you, Daniel."

"Me, too." Daniel raced out the door, jacket forgotten as he sang a new song.

"You're the child's father, aren't you?" The woman Blair had called Willie stood surveying him with watery blue eyes. "Anyone with vision can see that you're Danny's daddy. It's about time you showed up and took some responsibility. Now the first thing will be to get the child a decent home."

"Don't, Willie. Daniel isn't going anywhere. He's going to stay right here with me." Blair's chocolate eyes dared Gabe to say any different. "I've got things to do. Mac, you and Mr. Sloan no doubt have your *deal* to discuss. I'm going out.''

She was gone in a rush, those russet-tipped curls flying behind. Gabe stood and watched her through the window. He heard two voices speaking, saw an older man hug her close and kiss her cheek before the derelict old truck rattled down the road.

''She's not too happy with me, son. And I can't say I blame her. It was a nasty trick to play on my granddaughter.'' Mac's sad voice was resigned.

''Then why did you?'' Gabe could see no remorse on the lined, worn features.

''Because I love her. And I love that boy. I don't want to see either one of them hurt. I'm not as young as I was, you know. I'm afraid of what will happen to her when Willie and I aren't around for her to devote herself to. Blair is killing herself trying to look after us all.''

''Look after you?'' Gabe returned to his seat and thoughtfully sipped his coffee, aware that the ethereal Willie had drifted into another room. ''Why should she look after you? Are you sick?''

''Willie is, though she won't admit it. Her medicine costs something terrible. I've got a heart condition, but it's nothing serious. Not yet. As long as we've got my pension, we can manage, but what happens when I'm gone? Albert can only do so much.''

There it was again.

''Albert?'' Gabe fixed the older man with a severe look and waited.

''Albert Hunter. He's been our friend for years. Keeping busy around here is about the only thing that makes him forget the bottle. He's an inventor. Blair brought him home one day, asked me to help him sober up, and she's been taking care of him ever since. That's what Blair does—takes care of people. She needs to be needed."

"Oh." Gabe digested it all with a nod, his mind busy as he tried to merge this information with the woman he'd known. "Are you sure Daniel is my son?" he blurted. It was a stupid question.

Mac apparently agreed. He favored him with a severe look. "You know that right well enough, without me telling you. We were supposed to fly out Saturday morning for the wedding that night. But just as we were heading out the door, Blair phoned and said it was off. Next thing we knew, she'd dropped out of her last year of college. She came home at the end of October. Boy turns six at the end of May. You work it out."

Gabe didn't have to. He knew without doing the math. Hidden away in a trunk he hadn't opened in years was a picture his mother had put in an album just days before her death. His first day of school. He and Daniel could have been twins.

Gabe couldn't stop the questions. "Why didn't she tell me? Let me know?"

"Don't be daft, son! You pushed her away." Mac sniffed, his face scrunched up in anger, eyes blazing. "This is going to hurt her a lot, and I don't like to see my granddaughter hurt. Goes against everything I believe. The Rhodeses take care of each other. Always."

"So why drag me into your wonderful life?" Gabe couldn't stop the sneer from coloring his voice. This man would know soon enough that he wasn't the person to direct Daniel's young life. Gabe was totally wrong for that job. Suspicion dawned. Was this just another taker, the latest in a long list of people after his money? "What do you want from me?"

Mackenzie Rhodes fixed him with a fierce glare. "I want you to be a father to that little boy. It isn't right for him to grow up without a dad. Children need a man in their lives."

"What about you? And Albert?" Gabe almost laughed at the glower on Mac's face.

"I'm half dead! I can't be around for the boy forever, much as I'd like to. My rheumatism acts up in the winter so's I can barely get out of bed." He swiveled his arm as if to prove that it was damaged. "Albert's a good man, but he's not the boy's father. You are. Daniel needs someone to love and protect him and his mother. You owe him that."

No doubt he was right, Gabe conceded. He did owe the boy. But he couldn't be a father. He didn't know how. Even the prospect of it made him jumpy. Suddenly it was as if he was ten again and his dad was laughing at him.

"Swim, boy. Be a man."

Gabe could feel the doubts swirling overhead, waiting to cover him, to suffocate him just as the water had filled his lungs. He couldn't do this! He wasn't father material.

"I, uh, that is, I'm not..."

"Anybody can learn to be a father."

"But I don't..." Mac's steady gaze kept Gabe pinned to his chair, stopped the words that would express his doubts.

"You just have to look beyond yourself to someone else's needs." The wise eyes narrowed. "You told me in that letter your lawyer wrote that you wanted that land to build a house on. Said you were going to settle down, give up the city. That all true?''

Gabe nodded slowly, remembering his dream. A home of his own, a place to find out exactly who he was behind all the pretense.

''Why?'' Mac's back straightened.

''Why what?''

''Why does a big, important computer fella like yourself want to run away from his life?'' Mac tipped back in his chair and considered Gabe from that perspective.

''I'm not running away.'' Gabe wished he'd had some warning, some preparation for this inquisition.

''Aren't you?'' Mac munched on one of the cookies he'd appropriated from the jar. He handed the other one over. ''She can sure bake cookies,'' he muttered happily.

''Blair?'' Gabe waited for the other man's nod. ''When I knew her she didn't bake anything. She wore exotic outfits and crazy makeup. She reminded me of a butterfly whenever we went out.''

''You didn't know the real Blair. Never played dress-up in her life. She likes things casual, comfortable. So what about now?'' Mac's question was abrupt, to the point.

''She's still beautiful, but in a different way. She looks more fragile, and yet somehow stronger.'' Gabe tried to puzzle it out. ''I can't say it properly.''

''I wasn't talking about her looks. I was asking how you feel about my granddaughter.''

Gabe flinched under the scrutiny, his mind whirling a hundred miles an hour. ''I don't know. I don't know anything! How can I? All of a sudden I see a woman who walked out on our wedding years ago. And I find out I have a kid, a son I've never even heard about before. It's a little overwhelming.'' He frowned, his mouth as sour as if he'd just eaten a dill pickle.

Mac barked out a laugh. ''That's life for you. Want some advice? Get used to it. Fast. And make a decision.''

''A decision?'' Gabe frowned, wondering if the old fellow was hinting at something. ''What kind of a decision?''

Mac straightened, his chair banging to the floor with a snap that had Gabe flinching.

''Be a man! Figure out if you're going to break that boy's heart by walking away from him. Decide if you're gonna take on the role of father and be the best darn father any kid ever had, or if you're going to run away from your responsibility. Make a choice.''

For a moment, Gabe heard his father's tones, his father's mocking reminder that he'd never quite measured up to the standard. He surged to his feet, tension coiling inside him faster than lightning. And he'd thought running his company was pressure! ''I have to think.'' He spat the words out.

Mac shook his head as he set his cup on the counter. Then he turned and faced Gabe, his eyes tired, his expression sad.

''Don't know why I bothered,'' he muttered. ''Guess I figured you'd have some spunk and gumption and wouldn't let a woman do all the work. But, on second thought, you're not the kind of man my kin needs, Mr. Sloan. You like to run away from your problems instead of facing them.''

''Not true.'' Gabe shook his head. ''I like to figure out what the situation is before I make a move.'' He met that stern gaze unflinchingly, his voice cold. "And I'm not letting you renege on this contract. That land is mine." He patted his chest pocket and the paper beneath.

"Only if you build on it within the six months," Mac reminded him. "Anything else and the whole thing reverts back to me."

"I know that." Gabe pulled his boots on, then straightened and looked the other man in the eye. "I'll need to think it over," he repeated. "That's the way I do things."

Mac nodded, but his face showed worry. "Just don't run away," he ordered. "That doesn't do anyone any good."

"I'm not the one who ran. Blair did that, the day we were to be married." The bitterness still rankled. She'd dumped him, made him look a fool in front of his colleagues and associates, shown him up as a failure. He couldn't quite forgive her for that. Not even all these years later.

Mac's hand closed around his shoulder, his eyes piercing. "What other option did you give her?" he demanded quietly. "Blair loved you completely. I know that for a fact. She wanted to be your wife, she wanted the two of you to build a life together. She believed God sent you into her life, and she was ready to do whatever you asked of her. What did you do to spoil that?"

Gabe returned the stare, his temper sizzling. "I didn't do a thing any other businessman in my position wouldn't have done. If you knew anything about business, you'd know you have to protect yourself and your work. It didn't mean I didn't care about her. It was only a preventive measure."

Mac smiled sadly. "Protect yourself, eh. Who protected her, this young fiancée of yours? Did you?" The condemning words echoed around the room as Mac turned and walked away, his shoulders slumped in defeat.

There wasn't any more to be said. Gabe had failed then, and he knew it. He stepped outside, pulling the door closed quietly. He climbed into his truck and started it. As he left the house, then the yard and finally the valley, he couldn't help but admire the beauty laid out before him. It would be so nice to live here, to get away from the constant, petty demands on his time, to go back to just fiddling with things, daydreaming of new ways and means. He had only just begun to learn who was beneath the facade of successful computer designer. How could he take on a kid, do all the things a loving father should? Where did you go to find out how to love?

Gabe drove five miles into the minuscule town of Teal's Crossing and returned to his hotel room. Five minutes later he was lying on the bed, reaming out his lawyer.

"Why didn't you tell me about this goofy deal, Rich? I walked right into it. If I don't build a house here, I lose the land and the money. Whose interests are you protecting, anyhow?"

Richard Wellington was well used to his boss's anger. He snickered loudly over the line. "I *did* tell you, Gabe. At least six times. But you were so hung up on getting the plans drawn for this dream home that you completely ignored my warnings."

"And are they? Finished, I mean?" Gabe licked his lips at the mention of the plans he'd secretly reveled in for weeks. A place that would prove he was far more than anything his father could have dreamed of. A place that would show the world he didn't need any of them. A place he could hide.

"Ready and on the way to you by courier. Contractor says he'll start digging right away. Got some materials coming in the first of next week." Rich sounded very smug. "Pool should be ready right on time."

Those words sent a shiver up his spine, but Gabe ignored it. He'd deal with the past one step at a time. He couldn't ignore it any longer.

Gabe didn't know how else to broach the subject so he asked it straight out. "Rich, what happens if I get married?"

Silence.

"Well, uh, I guess you get a wife. Why?" The tentative response verged on suspicion.

Gabe swallowed, then dove in. "Remember Blair?"

Guarded silence, then a whoosh of air. "Yeah, I remember. Had you tied up in knots for months after she left town. Why?"

"She's here. It's her grandfather who's selling the land."

"Uh-oh." Papers rattled. "Why didn't I know that?"

"I don't know." He waited a moment. "She's raising my son, Rich." Gabe was stunned at the measure of satisfaction and pride he felt in saying those words. Son. Child of mine.

"What!" Rich burst into a volley of questions, which he proceeded to answer himself. Then he trotted out a list of things Blair could do to lay claim to the company, which he could prevent by suing for custody. "I'll have the papers to you in two days."

"I don't want to sue her for custody," Gabe murmured as an idea grew, taking shape and form in his mind. "I think I want to get to know my son. His name is Daniel."

"Daniel? Your father's name." Rich's voice was sharp. "How did she find out?"

Gabe smiled. Rich had learned distrust the hard way. Gabe had taught him all about it every time the young lawyer handled another deal. Now the man was as paranoid as he. The thought was not comforting.

"I don't know that she has found out anything. But that doesn't matter right now. I just know that this kid thinks he needs a father, and I can't turn my back on that. I remember what it was like too well."

"I suppose you do." Rich was silent for a long time. But when he finally spoke, his voice was filled with ominous warning. "Gabe, are you sure this child is yours?"

"Oh, yes. He's mine. That is not in question. Besides, Blair wouldn't lie." Though, if he remembered correctly, Blair hadn't told him anything about Daniel. His lips tightened. "So, buddy, how do I go about forcing her to let me get to know the boy?"

"You're sure you want to do this?" Rich's voice urged him to reconsider.

"I'm sure. His name will be Daniel Sloan, but he's not going to have a childhood like mine. Not if I can help it."

Rich appeared to accept this, for he offered no further objections. Instead his voice softened, bounding over the phone line with enthusiasm.

"I think you'll make a great father, Gabe. And

Blair always did worship the ground you walked on. If I remember correctly, she was ready to marry you. Why would she object to your presence now? I never did understand why she took off like that. You never said.'' A pregnant pause offered the opportunity.

Gabe swallowed, but he wouldn't lie to himself or his friend. He'd lived his life by dealing in cold, hard truth. He wouldn't stop now.

"It was my fault, I demanded she sign that prenup when I knew deep down that she wouldn't. I used her, Rich. I took her love and put my own conditions on it. And then I let her go as if it didn't matter. Yeah, she loved me once. I don't think that's going to be an issue now. She *might* agree to marry me, if I pushed it, but it would only be for Daniel's sake.''

He remembered her sad, mournful words when she'd phoned him the morning of their wedding day.

"I planned a white wedding in the church. My grandfather was going to walk me down the aisle. My great-aunt is bringing a big, showy cake. I was going to promise to love you forever. I was going to make sure we had lots of pictures so we could tell our children how happy we were.''

Gabe could still hear his caustic laugh. "Forever is in the movies, Blair. It doesn't happen in real life. And I won't be having any children. Not ever.'' He let her hear the steel in his voice. "I'm not the father type. That part is nonnegotiable.''

She'd gone silent then. He could almost see her face pinch tightly. Her voice, when it came at last, was soft, broken, brimming with tears.

"Goodbye, Gabriel Sloan. I love you. I'm sorry you won't believe that you're capable of more than making money.''

"Gabe? Gabriel!" Rich's worried tones kicked him to the present.

"I'm here." He sighed. "I don't think marriage is an option anymore, Rich."

"Are you sure you don't just want to sue for custody? Take the kid away. With your bankroll, you'd win hands down."

Daniel's bright, expectant face rolled into his mind's eye. Gabriel shook his head.

"Daniel's lived with her for over five years," he whispered. "She loves him and he loves her. I won't destroy that." *I just want to stay on the edges, feel the warmth, understand what makes a family.*

"Up to you, buddy. Okay then, if you're determined to get close to the kid, I guess the surest way is to threaten custody. If she's as good a mother as you think, she'd marry you rather than lose her kid."

Gabe laughed, but there was nothing amusing in the thought. "I don't think she'd ever marry me, Rich. And I sure can't marry her. You of all people know I'm not a family kind of man." He swallowed hard. "Six, almost seven years, but, after all, what's really changed?"

"Then you bluff. Threaten everything you can think of. I know you, Sloan. You'll think of something to make her see you're better suited to raising the kid than her."

Gabe hung up with the advice still ringing in his ears.

But you're not better suited, not at all. It's just another lie you let people believe, his conscience reminded him. *You couldn't possibly take that boy from the one person who loves him more than life. You have nothing to offer him. At least, nothing that really matters.*

"What do I know about being a father?" he whispered, worry overtaking his brain. "How can I be sure that I won't do something wrong? That I won't scar him or cause something that will make him unhappy years down the road, after I'm gone?"

It was a prospect he had to deal with. He knew how easily that could happen. His father hadn't wanted to leave his son the memories he carried. At least, Gabe told himself that, hoping it was true. But Daniel, Sr., hadn't been able to accept the son he'd fathered, either. Gabe simply didn't fit the baseball and fishing mold his father had set.

In fact, Gabe hated sports. All he'd ever wanted was to create things, to build things. To use his brain. Being sent to his room in punishment had provided hours of solitude to do just that.

"I won't force Daniel to be a replica of me," he assured his tired brain. "He doesn't have to like computers. If he wants to fish, I'll fish. I can learn that stuff. The company's okay, now. I've got all the money I'll ever need. I owe it to myself to take some time off—to see if Blair and I can make a go of it." He thought about Mac's letter. Why had it arrived when it had? Was God giving him a second chance?

"I owe it to him to do better than my dad did for me."

Which shouldn't be hard, given the past.

You owe him love.

That word sent a shiver of worry through his brain. Love? Gabe didn't think he had it in him. Not the kind of love the songs were about, the kind of love he'd read about in stories and poems. Certainly not the emotion that required you to give away everything you valued for the sake of someone else, the kind of love that made you vulnerable and weak, prey to others.

"He doesn't need to see that part of me," Gabe told himself. "He'll never know about that. I'll make sure of it."

But as he lay in his hotel room thinking about a black-haired little boy and his too solemn mother, Gabe wondered how he'd keep that shriveled-up, scared part of himself locked away when he'd spent such a large part of his life wondering where the next con to get his money would come from.

"One day at a time," he reminded himself. "With God's help, I'll face this one day at a time. That's what Pastor Jake said on Sunday."

Surely if you kept your eyes on the future, you couldn't get caught up in the past?

"Daniel's my only chance to make amends," he whispered, eyes closed as he prayed for help. "At least if I mess up, and I probably will, I know that Blair will make sure my son gets all the love he needs. He won't end up like me."

Please, God, don't let him end up all alone like me.

Chapter Three

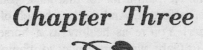

I don't understand how You could do this to me, God. Mac's always loved me, I know he has. Why did he have to find Gabe, send him that letter, stir things up? Why couldn't he have left well enough alone? Why did You let it happen?

Days later, and it was still a silly question! Blair knew the answer, at least the one Mac had given this morning when she'd asked.

"I'm old, honey. Some days I get tired and feeling down. I miss your gran, God rest her soul. Lots of times, all I want is to go to Heaven and rest, talk to God about things, give Myrtle a hug and kiss. But I couldn't ever die peacefully if I thought you and Daniel weren't cared for. It wouldn't be right."

"We're fine, Grandpa. We're managing really well now. I have the business and it's growing, Willie's doing better with those new pills and Albert hasn't had anything to drink since a year ago at Christmas."

Mac had snorted derisively. "Ha! You're lying to yourself, Busy Bee. We're scraping by and just barely doing that. What happens if the bees don't produce their usual this year? Or if some of those orders get canceled? We'll be in hot water then, and no mistake.'' He'd patted the pocket that held his bankbook with smug satisfaction. "At least this way I can be sure you'll have a nest egg to fall back on, and you've got the right to leave your hives in place for the next three years. He paid a lot for that land, you know.''

"He can afford it. And that's a bunch of baloney, Grandfather! You're as healthy as a horse! Selling that land to Gabe was just a way to manipulate him into finding out about Daniel, and you know it. I thought you loved us more than that.''

She fixed him with a stern look, but Mac didn't back down.

"It's because I love you two so much that I did it. You and Daniel need Gabe. And he needs a chance to be the boy's father. He's ready to move ahead with his life. Leaving the city and that company prove that. I think he's changed.''

"You don't know that, Mac. Gabe takes the company wherever he goes. And he doesn't *want* to be a father, not at all. It's just a duty thing.'' She shut off the piercing memory of that moment, that one single second of pure joy when he'd looked, really looked at Daniel, fully acknowledged that the child was part of him. She'd hoped to argue her case more fully. But Mac had shrugged and walked away.

Reality intruded as Blair dipped another taper into the wax and watched while it drizzled off, knowing that she was spoiling its finish by waiting so long. But today, business just didn't seem as important. She had to figure out what to do, decide how she was going to explain to Daniel that Gabe wouldn't be his father. Not ever.

"After all, he's had more than seven days to accept the idea. And he hasn't called, hasn't even spoken to Daniel. What kind of a father is that?"

No kind of father at all. Which was exactly why she'd never told Gabe about her son. He hadn't wanted to be a father, that much she was clear on. If she'd doubted it then, watching him avoid the children she worked with in her spare time would have been enough. And there were his words over the phone that last awful morning. *I'll never be a father*. The idea was repugnant to him!

The phone pealed a summons. "Hey, Blair!"

"Clarissa? How are you?" Blair grinned as she envisioned her formerly thin college buddy now hugely pregnant with the twins she'd been told to expect.

"I'm big, okay? Enough said." Clarissa's normally sweet voice halted, then continued. "I just read something I thought you might be interested in. Gabriel Sloan has handed over management of his company to a group of vice presidents."

Blair gulped, then nodded. "He's here, Pris. Mac sold him a piece of land, and he's apparently going to build a house on it. Some kind of castle affair, if the rumors are true."

Clarissa's voice wavered quietly down the wire. "Does he know?"

"About Daniel? Yeah, he knows."

Clarissa's mutter of protest left no room for doubt. She was mad. "They don't let women as big as me fly, Blair Delaney, but if you don't spill the beans,

I'll sic Briony on you. And you know how inquisitive she is.''

Blair giggled at the reminder of their friend and former college roomie, the third in their group who had also been dumped by her sweetheart. Bri had a scientist's mind. She liked the facts laid out clearly and concisely. She never accepted ''no'' for an answer.

''Nice try, Pris. But you can't. Bri's off somewhere in the Canadian Rockies doing the last bit of research for her thesis.'' Blair unplugged the kettle and poured herself a cup of hot water, dipping the lemon mint tea bag in and out rhythmically for several moments.

''I see.''

Blair waited, a tiny smile nudging the corner of her lips. Clarissa didn't disappoint her.

''Wade? I'll need the van. I'm going on a little trip to see an old college buddy who's trying to hold something back.''

''No, you are not traveling, Clarissa Featherhawk! You're staying right there.'' A mutter of threats rumbled across the line. ''All right, already! Gabriel Sloan arrived a few days ago. He's staying in the hotel in Teal's Crossing and he's tearing up my land as we speak. That's all I know.''

''Is he still as good looking?''

Blair closed her eyes, took a deep breath and admitted the truth. ''Yes.'' She let her mind brood on the ultra short raven's wing hair, the hard jawline, the full mocking lips.

''Does he still have those glacial green meltwater eyes?'' Clarissa demanded. ''I've never seen eyes that could turn such an aquamarine color. He used to make my knees shake when he looked at me.''

Still does, Blair wanted to yell. She quelled that schoolgirl response.

"I never understood why his Hollywood buddies didn't offer him a job. He's every woman's dream man." Clarissa giggled. "Except mine, of course. Wade's the one I dream of."

"Lucky Wade." Blair covered a rush of feelings by asking Clarissa innumerable questions about her pregnancy, her husband of almost one year, her ready-made family. Anything to keep the talk off of Gabe.

"You're stalling, Blair. Trying to throw me off the scent. That's always a good sign. I guess I'd better let you go so you can think about Gabe some more." Clarissa chuckled at her mumbled protest. "Keep me posted," she ordered before she rang off.

"As if there's anything to keep her posted on!" Blair said to herself. She emptied her cold tea into the sink and concentrated on work.

"So this is where you're hiding out?"

Blair whirled, shocked as much by the low, amused tones as by the sound of his rich, full voice echoing among the rafters of her bee barn.

"I wasn't hiding," she disagreed. "I have work to do. Unlike some people I could mention. Are all the little peons at Polytech too busy to miss you, Gabe?" She got back to dipping.

He didn't take offense. Instead he walked up and watched what she was doing.

"If you want the truth, they don't want me there anymore," he told her, a mocking smile tilting his lips. "It seems that I'm bad for their thinking. Their productivity goes way up when the boss isn't hovering around." He watched as her hands suddenly became busier with a series dipper that held six wicks.

"I didn't know you sold dipped candles, too. Can I try that?"

Blair frowned, but after studying his face, she found no hint of mockery. He looked genuinely interested in her work.

"I suppose." She showed him how to dip the wicks, then turn and redip to get the multicolored effects her customers loved.

Gabe tried several, lips pursed in concentration as he perfected the action. When she could stand the silence no longer, Blair took the rack out of his hand and set it aside.

"What do you really want, Gabriel?"

"I want my son."

Blair knocked the rack on the floor, completely ruining all her work. She ignored the mess and the expense as she stared at him, searching for an answer in his unfathomable stare. The words rocked her to the core of her being. Why, when she'd known it would come to this?

"You want Daniel? But you don't even know him!" She glared at him, daring him to deny it. "He's a little boy who's only ever known this place as his home. What kind of a father would rip him away from the only family he knows?" She chewed him out with her eyes, letting him see the contempt in them.

Gabe stayed where he was, his eyes watchful, swirling and slumbering with hidden menace as they studied her. "I don't want to take him away from you, Blair. I know how much you mean to him. I lost my own mother when I was young. I know what that's like."

She frowned. What did that mean, and why was he

suddenly opening up now? He'd never given her much insight into his past when they were engaged.

"I came to ask you something," he murmured at last.

"Go ahead. I reserve the right to refuse an answer." She wouldn't let him see her fear. *Please help me, God. Don't let him take Daniel.*

"Will you marry me?"

Blair wanted to laugh. Or cry. Something. Her eyes studied him, shocked by his quiet words. "Marry you? Why, for goodness sake?"

He looked innocent enough, his hands hanging at his sides, his feet crossed at the ankles as he leaned against the workbench in his natty designer clothes. Blair knew the pose was a disguise to conceal his thoughts. What was he planning?

"Why? Hmm." He frowned for a few minutes, then smiled at her, his eyes lighting up in the teasing glint she'd almost forgotten. "To keep a promise I made once, over six years ago."

"What promise?" She kept her gaze trained on him, refusing to fall for the diversion. "You never actually proposed. I did that, I think. You said okay." She looked away from his eyes, noticed the wax hardening on the floor. She bent to scrape it off the tiles, glad to avoid the speculation in his curious stare as the heat of a blush burned her cheeks.

"Maybe I didn't actually say the words, but I led you to believe that's what I wanted, too. Now it's pay-up time. So will you please marry me?" He waited till she'd straightened, then held out a black velvet box, and when Blair didn't take it, snapped it open to reveal a glittering marquise diamond set on a narrow gold band.

"Please, Blair?"

Blair's breath got tangled up in her throat, and she couldn't draw fresh air into her lungs. She stared at the gorgeous ring and wondered how he'd known she had always loved that particular setting. It wasn't what he'd chosen last time.

"I'm building a house, a home. That's why I bought that land from your grandfather. I'd planned to move here anyway. I'm leaving Los Angeles. For a while, at least."

"Why?" Her voiced croaked, her disbelief echoing around the room.

Gabe shrugged, but she could see him closing up against her probing, hiding his thoughts away, just as he'd always done. "Because I need to regroup, get a new game plan, figure out where I'm going from here."

She snickered, tossing the lump of misshapen wax into the garbage. "Yeah, right! You've always known that, Gabriel. Straight to the top. Business first. The biggest, the best, the brightest. That's always been your focus."

"It was," he admitted quietly. "But lately, it just doesn't mean as much. I feel like I'm missing something."

"So by marrying me, latching onto my son, you'll fill in some piece of your life that you didn't know existed seven years ago?" She shook her head, her ponytail flopping from side to side. "I don't think so. Thanks anyway, but we don't need your pity."

"It isn't like that." He sighed, leaning his narrow hips against her counter. He set the ring on the workbench as if it didn't matter a whit to him whether it got lost in the wax kettle or not. "Besides, he's my son, too. Why didn't you ever tell me?"

There was something in his voice, some plaintive yearning that made her stop fiddling with the wax and look at him.

"Would you have believed me?" she murmured. She could have wept at the hurt that darkened his eyes and made his lips pinch together. But it couldn't stop the questions.

"Can you guarantee that you wouldn't have tried to take him away or talk me into giving him up for adoption?" She made herself continue in spite of the torture contorting his handsome features. "You said you never wanted a child."

"That was before I knew, before I realized...." He stopped, brushed a hand across his eyes, scuffed a polished toe against the floor. "Maybe I'm just not saying this right."

Unreasoning anger flooded her.

"You've said everything you need to say. You've done your duty, Gabe. Don't worry, I'll tell Mac you offered. But no, I won't marry you so you can try out your hand at playing father." She saw his mouth tighten and hurried on.

"Daniel is the most important thing in the world to me. I love him, and I won't let you hurt him. You don't want a gold digger for a wife, or the encumbrance of a child in your life. Remember?"

When he winced at the repetition of his own words, Blair felt a stab of shame. But she wouldn't take them back. Daniel was too important to be used as a pawn, no matter how much she'd once cared for this man. She would not weaken, wouldn't let him see that she'd never given up the dream of a husband, and a home where she was the most important person in her husband's world.

"You're turning this around, Blair. Making it ugly. And that's not what I'm saying. I want us to be a...a family."

"Why?" She pressed him for an answer, knowing he wouldn't have one. Gabriel Sloan had never wanted any encumbrances in his solitary life. Things couldn't have changed that much.

"Because he's my son and I owe it to him," he said, exploding, mouth tight, eyes hard as emeralds. "And because you're his mother and I owe you, too. I should never have...never mind that." His cheeks darkened.

So he felt guilty for that one night of indiscretion? Blair smiled bitterly. Well, it was as good a reason as any to suggest marriage, she supposed. It just wasn't *her* reason, not the one she'd dreamed of, anyway. Not when she remembered her grandparents' marriage, and from what Mac said, her parents had been happy, too.

"So tell me, Gabe, just how would this marriage work?" She'd string him along, pretend she would go along with it. For a while. It would be interesting to note just how far the great Gabriel Sloan was willing to go with this experiment at nobility.

But in the end she would turn him down cold. Daniel was *her* son, and she intended him to feel the love in his life. Gabe didn't believe in love, and she couldn't forget that.

"Blair?"

She glanced up, then at his hand on her arm. Though he moved it immediately, Blair was only too aware of his touch and her reaction to it. How could she still feel this way? Especially now.

"I want the very best for Daniel," she began, trying to focus the conversation and direct it where she wanted it to go. "I know how much he's wanted a father. Especially lately. He keeps asking me about you, where you are, what you do, what you're like."

Gabe's face whitened. "He knows I'm his father?" His eyes were huge, his hands tight with tension as they clenched and unclenched at his side. "What have you told him?"

"He doesn't know *you* are his father." Blair fiddled with a tray of glitter that would accent the Christmas candles. "He doesn't know anything about his father. I've never said a thing."

"Then how—"

"They've been doing a series of projects at school about families." Blair shrugged at his frown. "This is a little community. Daniel knows the families of the kids in his class. He's seen two parents, a happy home, siblings. Some of the kids like to brag about their fathers." She shrugged. "I don't suppose his teacher thought of him as any different when they started on their family study unit."

"Which is exactly the scene you always wanted," Gabe muttered, peering at her. "Your ideal was always this happy home scenario, wasn't it? I can still hear you talking about how wonderful families were. I thought it was just a line."

And I can still feel how much you didn't want that. Blair searched for some underlying meaning to his words, but could find nothing to show he was goading her.

"Yes, well, we all have to grow up sometime. That

isn't going to happen for me. I've got Mac, Willie, Albert and Daniel to look after. I've learned to deal with my reality. The truth is, raising a child takes a lot out of you. I'm not sure I could handle any more of them.''

''Wouldn't it be easier if there were two of us parenting? I could take over sometimes when you needed a break. Or vice versa. We could share our son.''

It felt funny to hear him call Daniel that. And yet, Gabe *was* his father. He *owed* Daniel.

''We don't have to be married for you to be involved in his life,'' she offered, turning her back as she clicked off the switch controlling the wax warmer and began boxing already completed sets of candles. Surely she couldn't mess that up. ''If you're so determined to stay here, fine. Build your house. Live in it. You can see Daniel, be around for him. But his home will always be with me.''

''Why are you so dead set against marriage? Once you would have jumped at the chance.'' He stood opposite her, his hands mimicking her movements as he, too, boxed candles.

''I'm not against marriage, when it happens for the right reasons. You're mixing those reasons up just like you're mixing these orders up. You don't know the formula.'' She quickly redid the boxes he'd finished.

She wouldn't give in to the anger, wouldn't talk about the burn of distrust inside that still, after all these years, ate away at her. Let him think what he liked, she wasn't going to drag herself through it all again. She'd learned her lesson, learned it well.

Forgive and forget, Mac said. Very well. It had cost her dearly, but she'd forgiven Gabe. She had! But

Blair Delaney wasn't so stupid that she would ever forget the shame or the sense of betrayal he'd left her with. Not ever.

Gabe stood, staring at her with an odd questioning look.

"Sorry. Did you say something?"

"The formula for marriage?" A twisted smile tugged at his mouth. "You always did bring chemistry into everything."

His wink reminded her of the past they'd once shared. A past she didn't want to remember. She shook it off like a nasty pest and focused on his next words.

"What reason could be more right than providing a home for a child?" His voice remained calmly reasonable.

Blair sighed, then turned and walked toward her office. She wasn't going to get anything done as long as he was here. At least she could sit down for a moment, even if she couldn't relax.

One glance told her that Gabe had followed. He folded himself onto one of her small, ratty chairs and tilted back, his eyes intent on her.

"I know women grow up with this fairy-tale idea about weddings and marriage. Fine, you can have all the white lace and orange blossoms you want. I'll even hire a white charger if that will help. But the bottom line is that I intend to be a father to my son, Blair."

Blair studied him with narrowed eyes, her fingers knotting in her lap, where he couldn't see them.

"It would only be a temporary father," she argued angrily. "As soon as somebody from your office calls, you'll go trailing back. And Daniel will be left behind, wondering why you don't call him or take him to his soccer games. I'm not allowing that.'' She held his gaze, daring him to say what she saw glinting in the depths of his eyes.

''The thing is, you can't stop it, Blair. I *am* going to have my son.''

His mouth clamped in that implacable line she remembered so well. The emphasis was unmistakable. Blair could see the tiny white lines radiating from his lips and knew he meant business. *Oh, God, please make this stop!*

He leaned over and wrapped his fingers around hers, holding her hand carefully in his. Blair felt herself drawn by his eyes. Something glinted there, some shred of desolate rejection that she knew involved his past.

''I just want to spend some time with him, Blair. Is that so wrong?'' His voice softened, cajoled. ''You've had almost six years with him. I haven't had six minutes.''

There was no condemnation in his eyes, but Blair felt guilty anyway. She'd deprived Gabe of seeing Daniel's first smile, his first step, of hearing his first word. Little joys that parents should have shared. He'd been robbed of them.

''I don't want to take him away, Blair. Please believe that I don't want to hurt you. I just want to put the past behind us and make something good for the future. Something for Daniel.''

She tugged, and he let go of her hand, but stayed leaning across her desk, his face serious.

''Please? I don't want people gossiping about his parents, or the fact that we aren't married. I don't want him teased, mocked, ostracized. You said it yourself, it's a small town.'' He looked triumphant at having found this bit of wisdom to use against her. "Surely you wouldn't do that to an innocent child?''

Blair refused to trust in those softly spoken words. She'd trusted his honest intentions once before, and he'd disappointed her deeply. She wouldn't go that route again. Instead she cut to the truth of the matter.

"You're not in love with me, Gabe. You never were.'' She stated the facts baldly, ensuring that he knew she'd accepted the truth about their relationship.

"Wasn't I?'' He shook his head, his eyes hooded, shading his thoughts. "I don't know what love is. I was infatuated with you, that's for sure. For a while you made me believe things I'd never thought possible, sort of like a Tinkerbell in disguise.'' He grimaced at those words and tried again.

"I mean, well, I guess I felt more alive when you came into my life. I haven't felt that in a long time, Blair.''

It was an honest admission that she hadn't expected. But she couldn't allow it to sway her. Not now, not with Daniel to think about.

"That's nice of you to say, Gabe. But I don't want to base my son's future, my future, on something you *might* have felt a long time ago. It wouldn't be practical.''

He leaned back, his mouth tipped in a frown as he studied her. "When did you become so practical?''

She smiled, letting the sarcasm tinge her words. "A little over six years ago,'' she murmured, then felt ashamed as a flush covered his cheekbones. "I've had to be practical. Otherwise my family and I wouldn't have survived.''

Gabe jumped to his feet, shoved his hands in his

pockets and strode across the room and back. He stopped right beside her.

"Look, I know I messed up. I was a jerk, an idiot, a creep. You can call me whatever you want and feel totally justified. But I didn't know about Daniel! Now that I do, I want to try to make things right."

Blair sighed, more weary than she'd been in months.

"You couldn't just jet back to L.A., back to your company and your life there? You couldn't just forget about him?" She breathed out the wish with a hope and a prayer, knowing as she did that it was futile.

Silence reigned. She glanced up curiously and found him staring at her, his jaw clenched, his eyes roiling with anger.

"Could *you* do that? I'm not my father, Blair. I'm not going to ignore my son, dump him in his room and forget him there. I know firsthand what that kind of life is like."

"I'm sorry." She didn't know what else to say.

Gabriel Sloan had never shared his past with her, never allowed her to see into his childish hurts and disappointments. Oh, she'd had a few hints here and there, had known his adolescence had been less than perfect.

But this sounded like abandonment. Was that why he was so anxious to build a relationship with Daniel?

"I can't see how it would work." She fiddled with the pens jammed into the tin-can penholder Daniel had given her last Christmas. "I have to take care of my grandfather and my great-aunt. I can't just leave them to fend for themselves. They're old, they need me. Albert, too."

"So we'll include them." Gabriel's simple statement shocked her into silence. "It could work, I know it could. We'll make the house bigger, include a place for them in our family. I've never had a grandfather or any aunts."

"Gabriel, you've always lived alone. You don't know what it's like to have people around you all the time." Blair almost laughed at the idea of it. "Daniel isn't going to go away just because you're thinking up a new computer gizmo. He's a child. When he wants attention, he wants it now."

A thousand problems filled her mind, and yet she didn't voice them. She couldn't. Not when she saw the shimmer of hope that transformed his face into boyish eagerness.

"I'm not involved with any project. I hire people for that. Polytech almost runs itself now. Besides, that guy, Albert, is working on this neat idea. I checked it out yesterday. It sounds crazy, but I have a hunch...." Gabe's thumb rubbed his chin, his mind consumed with a new problem.

Blair smiled, remembering the habit from the old days. How many times had he taken her for dinner and started talking about his work, only to end up scratching diagrams on napkins and completely forgetting his surroundings?

"Gabe?" He turned from his perusal out her window, his eyes far away. "This is exactly what I mean. Just when you're in the middle of something, Daniel will come and ask you to play. Or Mac will need help with something. Or Willie will burst into your room and relay some insight that sends everything else out of your brain. This isn't your L.A. condo. You won't be able to get into your jet and take off to some spa in the valley whenever you want. Parenthood is a full-time occupation.''

He smiled, a huge, ear-splitting grin that begged her to share his exhilaration. "I know I'll have to make some adjustments." He rubbed his palms together as if he could hardly wait. "But I'll get used to it."

Blair scrambled for another route to dissuade him, frantically searching her brain. It was obvious Gabe was considering the idea of a family. She'd never have guessed that, and the knowledge made her question what other facets she'd missed in this complicated man.

"What would you expect from me? I mean, I've never been married, but I know I don't want to do it more than once. I couldn't do that to Daniel." She risked a glimpse at his face. "After all, we're not in love or anything. It wouldn't be the usual marriage."

Blair rearranged the items on the top of her desk again, her mind veering from the question she most wanted to ask.

"Blair?" He stood beside the desk, his hand stretched toward her. "Stop babbling and come here."

Blair looked at the floor, at her scuffed boots, at the messy desk, at her ragged fingernails. She looked everywhere she could until, finally, she looked at him. Then she slipped her hand into his and allowed him to draw her near him. Gabe's other hand clasped hers as he looked deeply into her eyes.

"It's not just Daniel I want," he murmured, his voice rippling over her taut nerves. "I think…I want all of it." He swallowed hard, his chest bulging as he took a deep breath.

"All of what?" She couldn't believe she was hearing this.

"I'd like the chance to find out what being a family means. I'm thirty-five, Blair. I know for sure what I don't want, and I think I know what I want. I'm willing—no, excited about making us into a family, including your grandfather, your aunt, even Albert. The more the merrier, as far as I'm concerned. I never had that, and I'd like to experience it. I'd like to prove that I'm not the selfish, egocentric swine my father was."

"But—" His fingers brushed over her lips, and Blair immediately ceased speaking. This was important. She had to hear what he was about to say. His voice was faint, hesitant.

"You have to understand something. I don't need anyone, Blair. I can go on with my life the way it was, and I'll be just fine. I could give you money, support you and Daniel, and you'd probably do a bang-up job of raising him." He made a sad little face. "But I don't want to do that. It would be like walking away, wimping out when I know I owe you both more than that."

He shifted, raked a hand through his shorn hair. Clearly the words made him nervous.

"I don't understand this family thing you've got going here. It's not part of my experience. You say I've missed out, that I don't understand. I'd like to. I'd like to be the kind of man your grandfather is. I'd like to have Daniel look at me the way he looks at Mac—as if the sun rises and sets on his shoulders." His hands gripped hers.

"It's hard to explain, but I'd like to give the boy the things a father should, even though I don't know what those are. I want to be there to see him grow up and explore his world.'' His fingers tightened. ''I'm not stupid. I can learn how to be a father. Maybe Mac will even help me. Just don't shut me out, Blair.''

She hesitated, her mind swirling with doubts. ''I don't know.'' He was obviously sincere, she could see that. But for how long?

''Please, Blair, give me a chance. Just say you'll think about getting married. I can wait, as long as you'll let me stay and get to know him. We can sort all the rest out as we go along. I promise I won't rush you, I won't push you, I won't abandon you. I just want to share Daniel with you.''

Stymied by his admission of need when he'd just insisted he didn't need anyone, Blair sought for something to say. It was tempting, so tempting. To be able to share Willie's medical bills with someone who could shoulder them, to have some of the burden of her money woes lifted, to know Daniel wouldn't be short-changed because of her childish mistake—it was all there for the taking.

Maybe it could work. Maybe she could have someone to talk to, to share the problems with. Maybe Gabe could be the man she needed, the father Daniel wanted. Maybe she just had to ask.

And that was the problem. Blair didn't ask for help. Not anymore. She was the one in charge, the person other people depended on. She couldn't relax that guard.

What was it he'd said? *Share it with you.* He'd sounded so forlorn, as if he'd never been able to share with anyone. And yet Gabe had been a member of the church, always chaired, hosted and funded a horde of projects, even spoken occasionally to the men's groups.

He's always stood alone among the crowd. The truth smacked her between the eyes. Was Gabe lonely?

"Well, Blair? Are you willing to do what we should have done years ago? Will you marry me?"

As she studied his resolute face, Blair tried to remember the cold, brusque businessman. She tried to recall his harsh words and the unflagging demands on his employees. But all she could see was a needy little boy who wanted a family around him—a man who wanted somebody to care for him, maybe even somebody to care about.

"I don't know," she whispered. "I have to think about this. And you should, too. It's a big step and it's irrevocable. At least for me."

As she said the words, she wondered if she'd done the right thing to let him hope. Daniel *did* need a father, but he needed a permanent one. Gabe wasn't permanent. Maybe, once he'd spent an evening or two with Daniel, he'd realize how demanding a child could be. Maybe he'd want to go back to his self-sufficient life. Blair shivered. Why did that thought bother her?

She wasn't prepared when Gabe leaned down and kissed her, his lips tender against her mouth.

"Please?"

She kissed him back. Partly because it was expected, but partly because she wanted to remind herself to be on guard. As the flood of emotion hurled through her body, she drew back and gazed into his eyes. She couldn't need him—not again.

"One step at a time," she cautioned. "We take it

very slowly. And we don't mention one word about marriage to my grandfather or to anyone else. You need to get to know Daniel. His needs come first.''

He threw back his head and laughed, his eyes sparkling like a glacial mountain stream tumbling joyfully over the rocks to freedom. Would fatherhood free Gabe? Or would it chain him to her for the rest of their lives?

''When?'' he demanded. ''When and how do I start being a father?''

Blair just stood there, her mind frozen as a picture of Gabe and Daniel together got caught in her brain.

''Right away,'' he decided, hugging her close, then setting her free. ''After school today. After all, it will soon be summer. He'll have lots of free time then.'' He stopped, considered, then glanced at her sideways. ''I want Daniel to have my name, Blair.''

Blair gulped. ''Uh, shouldn't we sit down and organize things first? I mean, you've got your house to build and I have my job. Eventually we'll have to tell the family so they can help. And Daniel.'' She closed her eyes, knowing how ecstatic Daniel would be to finally have a father. ''I need to prepare Daniel.''

Suddenly she realized what she was giving up. Daniel would no longer be solely under her authority. She wouldn't have the final say in his life anymore. She couldn't. If Gabe was to be an integral part of her son's life, Daniel had to learn to run to Gabe for some things, to depend on his father, to need him. Which was another reason to hold off this rushed marriage. The Gabe she remembered wasn't exactly dependable.

''Blair? You're not backing out? You're not going to change your mind, are you?'' His eyes shone like emeralds. He studied her, concern glinting from their depths. "You will share him with me?"

She shook her head. "No, I won't change my mind. I'm just thinking. Let's ease into it one thing at a time. Then we'll talk about marriage somewhere down the road."

"Not that far down. I want him to feel like every other kid in his class. Secure. Normal." His voice was firm. "I'm prepared to wait a month, two at the outside."

Her mouth flopped open. "Gabe, I can't! There's a lot to see to. A lot to think about."

He shook his head, his face implacable. "You'll dither and fuss, and it will never happen. Two months, that's as far as I'm prepared to go. Unless Daniel puts up some objection." He frowned at the idea.

"You're still issuing decrees." Blair fumed out loud. "I'm not promising anything, Gabriel. I want Daniel to have a chance to get to know you first. He has to be comfortable with this, or it isn't going to work. So does my family." She held her breath and waited, praying that she hadn't made a terrible mistake. "If our marriage happens, it will be because everyone is comfortable with it. Not because you force me into it."

Finally Gabe's dark head nodded his agreement. "Yes, maybe you're right. The community will have a chance to get used to the idea, too. And the house will be done."

"In two months?" Blair almost laughed. "I think you'd better be prepared to rough it out at the hotel, Gabe. It's going to take a lot longer than a few months to build the kind of house you're talking about."

"Where there's a will there's a way," he quoted gravely. He walked out of her office with a quick measured stride and returned moments later. "Keep this as a reminder," he murmured, holding out the diamond.

It caught her breath, sparkling and shimmering on his palm. But diamonds were for love. And he didn't love her. He never had.

Blair shook her head, wishing she could have at least tried it on. It was so lovely. She swallowed. "No. You keep it."

"If you don't like it we can get something else," he offered with a frown. "It's just that when I saw it, I thought of you."

"Willie would say that was God directing you." The brilliant stone caught the sun's rays and deflected them onto her shirt. "I've always loved this particular cut. And the setting is beautiful."

He let her admire it for a while. But when Blair finally glanced up, she caught a frown tugging at the corners of his mouth.

"I'll try not to mess up, Blair. I'm not very good at listening, but I promise I'll work on it." His voice brimmed with determination. "I think I could be a good husband and a good father. If I try hard enough." Before she could protest he slid the ring onto her finger. "Keep it as a symbol of our agreement," he murmured. "You can wear it when nobody's around if it makes you feel better."

"I'll try, too," she murmured, automatically threading her fingers through his out of habit. She ignored a noise from outside. "But I'll pray for some heavenly direction, as well. Just so we don't get off track."

He nodded. "Did you hear something?"

"Course she didn't. Thunderstruck by that ring, I imagine." Willie surged through the door, her austere face wreathed in a smile as she wrapped Gabe in one of her smothering hugs. "Knew as soon as I laid eyes on you that you were the man for Blair. 'Those whom God has joined together let no man put asunder.'" She smiled at his stunned surprise. "Plain as the nose on your face. Told Mac that yesterday."

"Yesterday? But…I only decided for sure last night." Gabe tilted his head as he studied the older woman. His eyes stretched wide in amazement.

Blair couldn't help the giggle that burst out even as she scorned her aunt's matchmaking.

"We're not getting married, Willie. At least, not just yet. So don't get too worked up. We want to let Daniel get used to his father first. Besides, Gabe might change his mind before the time is up," she warned, then gave up as Willie teetered on her tiptoes and smacked a kiss against Gabe's cheek.

Blair's eyes met Gabe's glittery ones. She shrugged in apology. "We're not the usual assortment of family members."

"No, we're better." Willie let him go and picked up Blair's hand. "When we love someone, we don't give up easily. That tenacity will be important to you."

"Busy Bee, have you seen Wil—" Mac burst through the door, then stopped as he spied the three of them. "Oh. What's going on?"

"These two are getting married." Willie glanced at Blair and sighed. "Eventually," she added. She frowned at Mac. "Well, don't just stand there! Welcome him into the family."

But Mac's eyes were scrunched tightly closed. No one could miss his whispered prayer. "Thank you, God! I knew You and I could pull it off if I could just get them together."

As she watched the two men shake hands, Blair frowned, remembering Mac's words. Time would tell if her grandfather had done them a favor or foiled any hope for the future.

Please help us, she thought while everyone chatted. *Please show me if this is wrong so I can stop it before it's too late. I have to be strong. I can't let myself need him.*

She glanced up, her eyes snagged by the look on Gabe's craggily handsome face. For the first time since she'd met him, he looked content. Why was that?

Chapter Four

"Daniel?" Two days later Gabe gulped, prayed for courage, then knelt in front of the little boy. "Could we talk?" He felt the hairs on the back of his neck prickle, felt the burn of Blair's eyes as she watched from the doorway. Oh, why had she insisted *he* do this? She was far more qualified. She'd given the boy enough hints that Gabe figured he didn't need to say more. If she was so worried, why didn't she tell him all of it?

"Whatcha wanna talk about? 'Lectricity? I got a book about that." Daniel rummaged through the bookshelves in his room, finally locating the tattered volume. He held it out proudly. "We're learning about this at school. I can read most of it myself."

"Really?" Gabe allowed himself a small diversion. "Did you know that I learned to read when I was about your age?"

Daniel's head came up with a jerk, and he stared at Gabe as if he knew something big was about to happen. "Oh."

"I guess it's only natural that you and I would learn to read early, you being my son and all." He held his breath and prayed for the wisdom to handle this properly.

"Yeah. Kids and dads have lots of things the same. Like our hair, 'cept yours is shorter." Daniel rubbed his hand over Gabe's shorn stubble. "An' you got eyes like mine, too. My mom's are a different color. Are you gonna stay my dad?"

Boy, the kid's mind was a maze. Gabe sucked in a breath.

"Yes, I sure am. Forever and ever. I bought some land from your grandfather, and I'm building a house across the valley." He waited for the questions.

"Dads usually live with their kids." Daniel's voice dropped to an almost-whisper. "Aren't you going to be staying around here? Is that why you need your own house?" He flopped onto the floor beside Gabe, the book forgotten.

"No, I'm staying. It's just that your grandpa's house is pretty full with him and his sister and your mom and you." He sat down and stretched his legs out, kneading the kink out of his knee as he searched for an explanation. "Besides, I have a lot of toys, and I need a special room for them."

"Toys?" Daniel scoffed. "Dads don't need toys."

"Oh, yes, Daniel. Everyone needs toys. That's what keeps our minds busy. My favorite toy is a big computer that I call Fred. I can do lots of stuff with him."

"Fred's a funny name for a computer." Daniel let that go, his mind obviously busy with something else. "Why did you wait so long?"

Gabe frowned. "Wait? What do you mean?"

"Felicia Cartwright gots a new baby in her house and its dad is already there. How come you waited so long to come and see me?"

Behind him, Gabe heard Blair walk into the room, felt the whoosh of air as she sank onto the carpet in front of him and folded her legs into the lotus position.

"It took Gabe a while to find you, sweetheart. He didn't wait on purpose." She picked up Daniel's chubby little hand and cuddled it between hers. "I'll bet he's really sad that he missed seeing you play hockey this winter, but I know he can't wait until you start riding Mortimer. Besides, your dad is here now. Is that okay?"

"Yes. That's what I prayed about." Daniel's big eyes widened, and a beatific grin spread across his face as he turned to his father. "Mortimer's a horse. Grandpa Mac says he's coming to stay on my birthday. Do you want to come to my birthday party? It's not for a while, but I could remind you."

Gabe had to swallow the lump in his throat. "I would really like that."

"Cool!" Daniel's grin drooped a little. "Are you sure you can stay that long?"

"Daniel, I'm going to live here. That means I'm not going to go away again, except maybe for a day or two to do business."

"Oh, you mean like when my mom goes to the big show to sell her candles? That's when Willie and me get to eat lots and lots of spaghetti. When we're full as a tick, Grandpa Mac does the dishes, and Albert cleans the floor. Making spaghetti is messy." He studied Gabe for a little longer. "Can you and me do things?"

"I sure hope so. I'd like to do things with you." Gabe shoved away the fear those words engendered. He would learn, he vowed. He'd learn it all. "There's just one thing, Daniel. I don't think I'm a very good dad. I've never been one, you see, and I'm not sure of exactly how to do it."

Daniel nodded sagely. "'Cause you didn't practice, right? Mrs. Jenkins says practice makes perfect. She's my teacher," he added in a confidential tone.

"She must know what she's talking about, then." Gabe made himself take a deep breath. "But just in case I do something wrong, you have to promise that you'll tell me so I can fix it. I want to be a very good dad."

Daniel nodded, then after a moment turned to play with his building set. Gabe sought Blair's eyes, wondering what to do next. She shrugged.

"Honey, are there any questions you want to ask Gabe or me? We'll try to answer the best we can."

Daniel glanced from her to Gabe. "What kinda questions?" he said.

"Oh, just things you might have wondered about. Things you don't talk about but would still like to know the answers." Blair spoke in an offhand tone, allowing the boy a chance to think his own thoughts on the subject.

Once more Gabe realized what a wonderful mother she was. She had a knack for knowing when to push ahead and when to back off, and he'd seen it at work in the past few days.

"I dunno." Daniel stopped what he was doing and cocked his head to one side. "What's his house gonna be like?"

Gabe understood this one. The boy wondered if it

would be full of don't-touch stuff. "I call it my castle," Gabe told him, grinning as the boy's eyes grew huge. "When it's finished, you'll be able to live there with the rest of us. If you want to see a drawing of it, I could show you that sometime."

"Wow! A real castle." Daniel jumped up and swung himself around the room in a series of acrobatic moves that had no name. They were the simple joyful outbursts of a happy boy. "I'm gonna live in a castle. Wait till the kids hear about this."

Gabe's glance flew to Blair. He caught the same stunned surprise in her face that he knew filled his own. Now what? he wondered. How was he supposed to handle this? Blair had been very clear in her insistence on a waiting period before she agreed to marry him. But how did you explain that to an excited five-year-old boy who'd only just found his father?

Mac's grizzled head poked around the corner. "What's all the racket up here?" he grumbled, a smile tugging at his lips. "Sounds like a herd of grumpy elephants."

"Grandpa, guess what? I'm gonna live in a castle with my dad." Daniel's eyes glittered with excitement.

"Is that right?" Mac's eyes moved from Gabe to Blair and back again. "Isn't that something? I suppose once you get all doo-dahed up in your fancy castle you won't want to come and see Willie and me in our rickety house?" He winked at Blair. "I'll be left all alone." His mournful face brought Daniel to his side.

"I'll always come and see you, Grandpa. Me and my dad are going to do lots of things together, but we could bring you and Willie to the castle, too. Couldn't we, Dad?''

The child's pleading gaze suddenly turned on his father, who was having trouble breathing after hearing himself called *dad*. ''Sure, sure we could,'' Gabe managed to say, trying to recall what he was agreeing to.

''And Grandpa can show us about fishing. Grandpa's the best fisherman in the world.''

''Danny, my boy, that's a wonderful compliment! Thank you.''

''Welcome.'' Daniel glowed as Mac patted him on the shoulder.

''But I think it probably takes a while to build a thing like a castle. Until it's done and everything gets sorted out, I think Willie and I will stay right where we are. We need to be around for Albert, you see. And I kinda like my own place.''

Daniel nodded as if he fully understood that sentiment. ''Me, too. Maybe I could have two homes.''

''Or three or four,'' Mac agreed. ''No reason why not. A house is just a house, but a home is a home because of the people in it. Doesn't really matter where it is or how fancy it is. What matters is how much love there is inside it.''

''I know, Grandpa.'' Daniel's hand slid into the blue-veined grasp, his fingers wrapping around the gnarled, bent ones. ''An' we got lots and lots of love, don't we? We can make anyplace be home.''

Mac bent over and kissed his tousled head. ''That we can, laddie. Now maybe your mom and dad need some time to talk about things. How about if you and I go check out the creek? It's getting pretty high, you know. Albert's been trying out a new gizmo that counts how many fish go down the stream. Do you want to see it?''

"Yes!" Daniel danced from one foot to the other. Then he glanced at Gabe. "I can't do nothing with you right now, 'cause Grandpa and I gotta go look at somethin'. Maybe after lunch. Okay?"

Gabe tried not to laugh. "Very okay," he agreed. "I've got a few things to do myself."

"Cool." Daniel dragged his grandfather out of the room, talking a mile a minute as he went.

"Cool. The word of the week." Blair smiled, but there was worry lurking in the depths of her coffee-bean eyes.

"Thanks for stepping in." Gabe said it sincerely. "I got a little flustered there for a minute. He might look like me, but his mind works like yours, twisting and turning all over the place."

"Gabe, how long is it really going to take to build that house? I'll have to try and put it in some kind of time frame that he understands." She got to her feet, her eyes moving to the window.

"Don't look smug, but the two months has been extended. They've now promised no longer than nine weeks, and I guarantee they won't go beyond that because they'll forfeit a huge amount of money." He checked to make sure she wasn't laughing. "That puts us around the end of April. Might take a few days to get some furniture and stuff, but I'd think we could move in by the end of the month. Does an early May wedding suit you?"

"You're intent on going through with this?"

He nodded. "Oh, yes. I intend to go through with all of it." She stood there studying him, so Gabe got up and wandered to the window. This was a nice enough site, but he had the better one, especially with that creek running alongside.

He heard the whisper of her movements, knew the exact moment when she stopped behind him.

"Are you positive? You're not missing the company?"

Gabe turned, wondering at the funny sound in her voice. A certain huskiness that usually meant she was emotional. But why?

"I told you, the company will do just fine without me. I'm not needed there. Not anymore. My staff is trained to handle almost anything." His breath caught in his throat when a hint of her perfume snagged on the breeze and wafted past him. A little bit spicy, a little bit flowery, very soft. It personified Blair, and Gabe suddenly realized that he'd never forgotten even that small detail about her.

"What's really bothering you, Blair? I've seen you giving me these little sideways looks when you think I'm not watching. What's going on inside here?" He tapped the tumble of curls she'd fastened to the top of her head with a huge yellow clip.

"You won't like it," she warned.

"Probably not." If he knew Blair she'd blurt it out full speed, without worrying about his sensibilities. She was hopeless at prevarication. "Go ahead."

"It's not a criticism. You've done very well with Daniel. Better than I ever expected. It's just…well, I didn't expect you to fall in with Aunt Willie or Mac so easily. I kind of thought you and Albert had things in common, but Aunt Willie is different."

"She's a breath of fresh air. I can't imagine how anyone can't love her. She's like you." Blair's tiny frown made him smile. "She never lies or pretends what she doesn't feel. She doesn't try to stroke you."

"You always did despise that. Come on, let's get some coffee and relax on the veranda." She led the way to the kitchen and poured out two cups.

"I hate it because it's deceit. I can deal with somebody's anger or dislike, or most of the other stuff. But when they sweet-talk out of one side of their mouth while they stab you with the other, well, I get mad." He took a sip of the potent black brew and shuddered. "What do you people do to get it like this? It tastes like sludge."

Gabe emptied the pot and set about making a fresh one. When it was streaming through the filter, he turned to study her. "There's more, we both know it. You might as well say it, Blair. I can take it." He hoped.

"I wish you wouldn't listen to Mac so much." She let him take her cup, pour a fresh one.

"You don't like me to talk to your grandfather?" Gabe filled his mug and sat down. He tried to figure it out, tried to keep his cool. "Why not? What do I do that bothers you the most? Am I upsetting him or something?"

She wouldn't look at him, wouldn't meet his gaze. Worry snickered through Gabe. What had he done that was so awful? Was she going to rescind her offer about Daniel? Was she going to make him leave?

"Just say it, okay, Blair? You don't want me around them. You want me to go." Despair tugged at him, dark and overwhelming. He wouldn't stay where he wasn't wanted. He'd go. But just until he'd figured out something else. There had to be a way for him to be a part of this family. There just had to be.

Blair opened her mouth, but clamped it shut when her aunt breezed into the room clad in a frilly dress with big red polka dots and flounces that fluttered as she moved. It was something straight out of the good old days.

"Hello, darlings!" Willie picked out her favorite china mug with the sprigs of lavender painted on the sides. "I smelled freshly brewed coffee and, after our tête-à-tête yesterday, I knew it had to be yours, Gabe dear. No one else makes coffee as well as you. Thank you." She bent to ruffle his hair, her fingers gentle as they brushed his neck and over his shoulder. "I do love it when you come over."

Gabe squeezed her fingers and brushed a kiss against the powdered porcelain cheek she presented. "Thank you, Miss Rhodes. I appreciate the way you've accepted me into your home. I hope I'm not intruding. Mac told me you're preparing for a play."

"Darling, you're our Blair's almost-husband! And my almost-nephew. You belong here. As soon as I get that attic cleaned up, you can move in. Or were we moving out? That medicine gets things all muddled in my mind. I forget." She leaned to hug him close, covering him in a cloud of lilac fragrance. "Oh, well. Yes, I'm doing a bit piece in *Hamlet* with our little theater group next month. I hope you'll come."

"I wouldn't miss it." He watched her exit, then resumed his study of Blair. To his amazement, she had a frown on her face.

"I wish you wouldn't do that," she mumbled.

"Do what?" He was almost afraid to say it, afraid to hear her response.

"Get so friendly with them. Make them think you're always going to be here, that they can count on you." Her mouth clenched white, and her eyes flashed with anger.

Gabe's jaw dropped.

"Oh, don't act so surprised. You know what I mean. Letting them believe that everything's going to be wonderful."

"Isn't it going to be?" He challenged her to deny it.

"No. Yes. I don't know! You don't know, either." She ladled another two teaspoons into her already sweetened coffee. "You haven't been here long enough to know, and I wish you wouldn't keep up this pretense of loving the jolly backwoods. It's a lie, and we all know how much you hate lies, Gabe."

She was jealous of his bond with her family! Gabe breathed a sigh of relief. This at least he understood. If he had a family like this, he'd be jealous of somebody butting in, too. He followed her to the veranda.

"I'm not pretending or lying." He waited till she was seated, then took the chair beside hers. "I do like it here. It's so natural, so beautiful. Yesterday I saw deer. I didn't know there were any still around."

"The neighbors have a game farm." Blair wasn't slouched in her usual relaxed position. She crouched on the edge of her chair, like a cat ready to pounce. "And don't change the subject. You know very well that this isn't your usual setting. It's hokey and so totally *not* your style."

Gabe felt like a rabbit caught in her headlights. But for once the scrutiny didn't bother him. Let her study him night and day. He didn't mind. He wasn't pretending a thing. He loved it here. He'd never felt so comfortable around anyone as he did with this family.

"What are you getting out of this, Gabe? A good

laugh? A little payback? What?'' Her eyes dared him
to respond.

He couldn't tell her the truth. He couldn't explain
that what he got here was unadulterated acceptance.
Nobody thought it was the least bit strange when he
sat in the barn and worked on his laptop for hours at
a time.

Yesterday, nobody had called him a geek or raised
their eyebrows when he forgot to get out of his car.
He'd been so wrapped up in the idea for a new game
that he'd scribbled as much as he could on paper. He
remembered Mac brought him a sandwich and some
chicken soup that he'd forgotten to eat. When it got
dark, Willie came and tugged on his arm until she
lovingly captured his attention.

"What makes you think I'm getting anything out
of it, other than a chance to see my son every day?''

She sniffed. "As if you even notice him! I had to
pry you away from that Fred thing to get you to kiss
him good-night,'' she grumbled. "I could feel you
itching to get back to it when Mac coerced you into
that game of rummy. The way you look today, I'm
pretty sure you spent most of the night peering at it.''

"I did.'' He admitted the truth freely. "I got an
idea for a new game.'' Gabe made himself shut down
on that. What woman, newly engaged or otherwise,
wanted to talk about computer gizmos? "But it's
nothing I can't change. I just have to learn how to do
it.'' He hunkered down, relaxing, his chin on his
hands, elbows on his knees. "I'm not trying to steal
them, Blair. They'll always love you best.''

"What?'' She stared at him. "I'm not jealous, you
idiot! I just don't want them hurt.''

"Neither do I. Believe me, that's the last thing I

want. I think they're very special.'' He followed when she jumped up and scurried inside, pausing at the counter while she rinsed her cup. ''I know you're looking out for them, Blair. I remember those little envelopes you used to mail every other Friday. Special delivery, priority. They were to them, weren't they? To help out? Even then you were taking care of them. Just like you always take care of everyone around you.''

''Oh, brother!'' She lunged away from the counter, but Gabe moved and blocked her escape. She glared at him. ''You make me sound like Mother Teresa or something. I'm not a saint, Gabe. I just don't want to see them hurt. They're my family.''

''I know.'' He leaned down and brushed his lips against hers, remembering the fire of her kisses from long ago. But this Blair was wary, more reserved. She stepped away from him.

''I have to go to work,'' she said softly. ''Thanks for the coffee.''

''You're welcome.'' Gabe watched the screen door wheeze closed. He saw her stop and listen to Daniel and Mac talking to Albert. Gabe walked outside, hoping to overhear their conversation. Maybe if he listened to them together, he'd get a better idea of what kids did with their fathers, what families talked about.

A wave of lilac assaulted his nostrils as a delicate hand ruffled his hair. Willie's barely audible voice floated to him. ''She's very protective.''

Gabe jerked upright. He couldn't remember when anyone had ruffled his hair. Not ever. Tears burned in his throat. Why? he asked himself. Why did that little touch mean so much?

"Blair's made herself into our guardian. She talks a tough line, but inside she's afraid."

"Blair? Afraid? I don't think so." Gabe turned his head to stare at the willowy woman on teetering heels who seemed more like his almost forgotten mother every day.

Aunt Willie was adamant. "If you knew her better you'd see it. She's always trying to make up for something, go the extra mile, ensure she's done more than anyone would ever expect. She's trying to atone for her sins."

Gabe blinked. "Huh?"

"It's true. She's been like that since her parents died when she was four. I believe that deep down, Blair thinks that if she'd been better, more lovable, done more, said more, helped more, that her parents wouldn't have died. Somewhere inside she still clings to those beliefs. So she stretches herself thin trying to make up for her mistakes. She doesn't understand grace."

"Grace?" Gabe felt like a recorder, repeating whatever he'd heard.

Willie waved him into a chair while she made herself comfortable in her willow rocker.

"Grace," she asserted firmly. "It means something that's given freely, something you can't earn or deserve. It's like God's grace to us. We're sinners, all of us. We've done nothing to deserve His love. In fact, we should be punished. And yet God says, 'It's all right. I forgive you. I gave My son's life—I don't need yours. You're forgiven, no strings attached.' You see?"

Gabe nodded slowly. "I've heard about it, and I

guess I understand it when it comes to God. But I don't see why you think Blair's stuck on it.''

"Because she doesn't believe that she can just accept forgiveness." Willie lifted her knitting from a bag nearby. Her needles clacked rhythmically. "She thinks she has to pay, that she's too far for grace to reach."

"But what could she possibly have done that gave her such an idea?'' He closed his eyes and listened to the song-drenched breeze as birds flitted in and out of the valley. He felt the sun on his face, warming him, the wind caressing him. And he waited for Willie's answer.

When it came, it drove every other thought out of his mind.

"Blair went against everything she believed in when she slept with you. She wanted to obey God's commands and keep herself only for her husband, but she made a mistake. When she became pregnant and had to drop her studies to return home, she believed it was because she needed to pay for her sins." Willie riveted him with her steady stare. "She's trying to atone for a mistake that's almost seven years old.''

Chapter Five

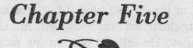

A month later Gabe sat on the Rhodes's veranda again, but his thoughts were no clearer. He couldn't get Willie's words out of his mind, though he'd yet to face Blair with them.

The guilt gnawed at him. *He'd* done that to her. He'd made her abandon her beliefs, her principles. He'd been so desperate to hold onto her love, he'd rushed her, forced her into something she wasn't ready for. He'd taken it all away, and then added insult to injury with that stupid prenup. The guilt was his, not hers. He wanted to tell her that, to atone for it, to wipe her slate clean no matter what it did to him.

And yet, he was afraid to show his emotion. Afraid that if he let her see how much he wanted to keep what he had, how much he treasured the security of sharing this family with her, told her how inconceivable he found it that he could come and go at will and still be welcomed back, she'd take it all away from him.

Their mistake was in the past. Wasn't it better to leave it alone?

"Hey, Daddy, want to come fishing? Grandpa and me are going." Daniel stood in front of him, his knobby knees sticking out under the shorts he'd reluctantly donned when the weather had turned unseasonably warm.

"Son, I'd just love to go fishing. But maybe later on, okay? If this weather holds." Gabe swung the boy up and around, delighting in the squeals of laughter that resulted.

"You'll get his lunch all over him if you keep that up." Blair's voice held a hint of warning, and Gabe instantly set Daniel down. "How's the house?"

He turned to face her and sucked in a breath at her beauty. She wore no fancy clothes, no brand-name outfit. She had on a sleeveless white cotton blouse and a pair of denim shorts that left lots of golden brown leg bare to the sun. Her hair was caught up in a fluff of tumbling curls, bursting from two combs that followed the cap of her skull. Her bangs, long and wispy, curled with perspiration, and she swiped them off her forehead with a careless hand. The hand that wore his diamond.

"You're frowning. Is the place that awful?" She winked at him. "Did the castle thing turn out to be a bad idea?"

Gabe's heart relaxed as her chocolate eyes melted with laughter that spilled onto the lazy afternoon heat. For some reason, she'd refused all his entreaties to look at the progress he'd made. She'd sent Mac to check her hives and add more of the funny boxes she called supers. But she stayed away from his field.

Gabe didn't know why, but he had a hunch it had to do with trust.

"It's not exactly a castle," he told her. "Everything's moving very well. You'd know if you came and looked at it yourself." He dared her to refuse.

"Oh, I will, one of these days. Things are just so busy right now. And it has to be a castle if it's home for a computer king." She ignored his pleading look and turned to the house. "Gardens and flower beds wait for no man."

"You know very well they're both finished, for now." Willie shoved the door open with one foot, balancing a tray that carried a frosty pitcher of lemonade and six glasses. "Do you good to get out and relax for a while."

"No time like the present." Gabe added his two bits to the conversation. Not that it would sway her. She ignored him when she could, when he'd let her get away with it.

"Mommy, could we please go see the castle? My daddy's building it specially for us an' I want to see it. Please?"

The voice wheedled and whined, begging so sadly that Gabe wondered how Blair could keep from yelling her agreement. No doubt she was a far better parent than he'd ever be.

"All right, we'll all go. After I take a break and have some of Willie's lemonade." She tossed Gabe one stark, meaningful glance before moving across the veranda to lean on the balustrade. "You guys could have gone anytime, you know," she said, watching her grandfather climb the stairs.

"We wouldn't dream of looking at your future home without you present. Come on, Albert. Come and have a drink. Leave that contraption alone for a minute!"

Albert straightened slightly and pushed the gray strands out of his eyes before nudging his glasses up his nose. He looked like a tired old professor. "Oh. Yes. Of course." He darted up the steps like a rabbit pursued, accepted his glass of lemonade and drained it in one gulp. "Delightful. Thank you. Must be going now." He limped down the steps, favoring the leg Gabe knew he'd injured in the war.

"Albert?" Blair's soft voice stopped him mid-step. "We're going to take a look at Gabe's castle. Wouldn't you like to come and take the grand tour with us? We won't be long. After all, you'll all be living there one day, too."

"*Our* castle," Gabe muttered, but no one paid him any attention.

"Yes, of course. Lovely." Albert scurried across the grass toward his work shed, mumbling to himself. Halfway there, he stopped, turned around, a frown on his face. "Castle?"

"We'll come and get you when we're ready to go." Willie nodded when he stared at her for a minute. Then Albert gave a stiff little bow and resumed his stumbling gait to his workroom.

"What's he working on now?" Blair turned to Gabe, her manner telling him that she didn't want to ask but felt compelled to do so.

"A kind of dune buggy thing that's used for retrieval." Gabe accepted his glass with a smile at Willie and in return got an affectionate caress as her hand tenderly cupped his cheek.

"Surely that's not new?" Pointedly, Blair took a seat several feet away from him.

"It is when it's for use in the Arctic." He felt a smug ping of satisfaction at the startled looks on their faces. "It has every chance of succeeding, too. The parts are specially insulated so that they don't seize up when it's cold." He waited, and when no one spoke, looked directly at Blair. "Are you ready to go now?"

She set down her glass. Gabe reached out and pulled her from her chair. "I hope you like it." He couldn't help gazing into her lovely eyes. "If you don't, just tell me. At this stage we can change almost anything."

He could see the hesitation there, the words unspoken. "Almost anything," he repeated quietly, reading the unspoken words. "I'm not leaving, Blair."

A touch of sadness clung to him. This should be a happy time, a time they looked forward to. This, after all, would be their future home. Instead Blair's eyes swirled with secret fears and her fingers clenched in worry. She still didn't trust him. Not yet. But she would. Gabe was determined to prove himself.

He knew nothing about families, even less about unity and drawing together. But he could learn. If he just worked hard enough, he knew he could learn.

"It's beautiful." Willie spun around in the huge kitchen with its modern hearth. "Look at this, Blair. The breakfast nook is part of the turret. Those windows! My goodness, the morning sun will just light this place up."

"I like the dungeon." Daniel grinned at his father. "It makes me think of pirates and things."

"It's not really a dungeon, son." Gabe mussed his hair just as Willie had done his own. "It's a workroom. I'm going to be building some things down there.''

"Can I help?" Daniel's big eyes pleaded for the chance.

"Of course. Albert's going to help, too. We'll call it the invention dungeon. How about that?"

Mac flopped onto a short ladder left behind by some workman. He thrust out one hand and grinned a huge, smirking grin. "I don't know how you've done it, boy, but you've certainly done it. This place is shooting up faster than a geyser in Yellowstone."

"Most of it was prebuilt to specs. It just needed a few alterations, then it was shipped in and assembled once the foundation was solid. I used those straw blocks for a lot of it. Good insulation in the winter and just as efficient in the summer."

Daniel peered through the windows that overlooked the back yard. The rough terrain had been torn apart by huge earthmoving machines, which had left a cleared space. But the creek and many of the trees still stood firm and untouched.

"What's that?" he demanded in a shrill voice, breaking through the conversation.

"Daniel, don't yell. Ask politely." Blair turned toward him. "I've been wondering that myself, Gabe. Why is that hole there?"

Gabe swallowed hard. "It's going to be a pool."

Willie clapped her hands in excitement. Mac whistled. Albert went out to take a closer look. But Blair stood there, her eyes dark and curious.

"I didn't know you swam. I know you had your club and that you lifted weights or something. When we used to go to Santa Monica pier, you always insisted on staying on the beach." Pink streaks shot across her face. "Of course, that was a long time ago."

Gabe went for honesty. "I can't swim," he told her.

Blair frowned in perplexity. "Then why?"

"I'm going to learn." He shut out his father's mocking voice and faced four sets of curious eyes. "It's just something I have to do."

"And you couldn't do this in the community pool? You had to build your own?" Blair shook her head in disbelief.

He knew she thought he'd gone to excess on some things, but Gabe didn't care. This was going to be his home, and he wanted it to be perfect for everyone. Then maybe she would stay, settle down. Relax and build a future with him.

"It might take me a long time to learn. I didn't want to hog it." *Or have everyone gape and stare while I have a panic attack.*

"I might just take those lessons with you." Mac shoved himself upright and grinned. "Never did learn even the dog paddle. 'Spect I could take a dip or two with you. But not in winter. I draw the line there."

Gabe couldn't stop his mouth from spreading in a grin even if he'd wanted to. This was what he liked about them. No questions. Just acceptance. If he wanted to stick a big pool in his back yard, well, they embraced that just as they embraced him. No problem.

"I'm going to heat it, Mac. Maybe we could enclose it. You know, have an underground tunnel to the house, or something?"

"You can do that? You don't say!" Mac clapped him on the back. "Thought of pretty near everything, haven't you, son?'' He shoved his hands in his back pockets, teetering on his heels. "I can always go to the old place to do my whittling. Wouldn't want to mess up this castle."

Gabe pointed a finger. "There's a workroom right over there if you want it, Mac. I had it put there specially. That way you won't have to take the stairs to get there." While Mac and Willie enthused over the room, Gabe moved closer to Blair. "Do you want to come and see the master bedroom?" He kept his voice diffident, absent of meaning so she wouldn't panic.

"It's on the main floor?"

He nodded and led her out of the kitchen, through the adjoining family room and the solarium to the rooms he'd insisted on designing himself.

"This is the bedroom, walk-in closets, bathroom. The Jacuzzi is through there, and there's a steam room, too."

"You'd think you were addicted to water," she muttered. "If the tub upstairs was a foot longer, you wouldn't have needed the pool." Her eyes were huge as she studied a tub set on a higher level against a bank of opaque windows. "Does this open?" She tried one and found that, indeed, it swung out onto a flagstone patio that was surrounded with a bounty of trees and flowering shrubs ready to be planted. At one end lay the beginnings of a rose garden.

Gabe spared a glance to notice that they'd already planted a few of the prickly bushes. He turned to the room he'd planned so carefully, then adjusted after she'd quietly agreed to marry him late one night last month.

"This will be a two-sided fireplace," he told her,

motioning to the roughed-in area that snuggled against one end of the hot tub, while the other looked over the bedroom. "Is it okay?"

He was beginning to worry. She hadn't said much, just walked around, touching a hand here, a finger there.

"It's very...romantic." Her voice whispered across the silence. "But I don't need it. I'm not a fancy person, Gabe. I'm not the socialite deb you thought I was. I'm a working woman, a mother, a plain, ordinary person. This is so—" she waved a hand, taking in the rich cedar beams, vast amounts of window space and glistening amenities "—so *much*. I don't need all this, Gabe."

He grinned. She was worried about spending a lot of money. He could handle that.

"Nobody *needs* this, Blair. And it won't bring us happiness or make us any more satisfied. There's always bigger and better. I know that." He tried to put it into words without letting her see the shadows that still lingered from so long ago. "But I wanted something special. I've never had a home, remember?"

"But your condo? What about it?" She sank down on one of the steps that led to the Jacuzzi and, after a moment, Gabe sat beside her. "It wasn't anything like this."

"It wasn't home. It was a stopping place. I needed a place to sleep and it did the job." That was all it had been. The knowledge hit him with amazement. It didn't have the warmth, the welcome that Mac's little farmhouse offered, in spite of the ridiculous cost.

"Gabe, don't take this the wrong way, okay?" She laid a hand on his arm in supplication, her dark eyes glowing in the fading light. "You've gone to a lot of trouble here. And a lot of expense. You already know how much I love swimming. And that jungle gym area you had set up for Daniel is wonderful. I know he'll enjoy it, but…'' Her voice trailed away, her forehead furrowed. ''It's too much,'' she finished at last. ''I don't want him to become, well, jaded.''

''You mean jaded like me?'' It hurt to have her say such things, but he needed to get it out into the open.

''No.'' Her head swung slowly, thoughtfully from side to side. ''I don't think you're jaded. But a lot of your friends were. They had no pity left for a home-less person or a fellow who was down on his luck. They couldn't see past their own selfish lives to the bounty they enjoyed. I don't want Daniel to grow up like that. I want him to understand that love is more important than any of that.''

Gabe thought about the little boy for a moment and let his lips turn up at the remembrance. ''I think Dan-iel already has that fact firmly established. And I'm not trying to buy his affection, Blair. Please don't think that.'' Her hand was still on his arm, sending little prickles of heat straight to his chest. He shifted a bit so that he could entwine his fingers with hers. ''Maybe I'm not saying this properly.''

''Just say whatever's on your mind.'' Her perfume, soft and enticing, drifted across to him. ''I'll try to understand.''

He studied her beautiful face for a moment, then gave in to temptation and told her what was in his heart. ''I don't know anything about building a fam-ily, Blair. I never knew what that was like. But, I think it's what I want.'' He swallowed hard, then pushed on.

''I thought if I could get this part of it right, the

building, the rooms, the places for everyone so they'll be comfortable here, well—'' he stopped, hating to go on, to show how much he needed her to help him with this ''—I figured maybe you could do the rest of it.'' It came out in a rush.

Blair frowned at him, curling tendrils of her glossy hair tumbling about her face and down her neck. ''I could do what?'' she asked in confusion.

''The family part. Or at least, you could teach me. You and Willie and Mac. You're good at it.''

Her fingers tightened around his for just a moment. He stared at them, then looked into her eyes. To his surprise she had tears glistening on her lashes.

''I can't make us a family, Gabe.''

His heart sank to his heels at the death knell of those words. His head dropped to his chest. He'd known, deep down, that it couldn't work, that he was asking too much, giving too little. Blair didn't care about money. He'd always known that, though he'd pretended otherwise. Why would she be any different now? Why would his castle make any difference to her feelings for him?

''I understand.'' He eased himself away from her, preparing to get up as he loosened his fingers and let hers slip away. It was just like his dream—slipping out of his grasp.

''Gabe?''

He froze, preparing himself for her chastising. ''Yes?''

''No one person can *make* a family. It's a give-and-take relationship. And it takes time. We can't just automatically be a family because you want it.''

''I know.'' He didn't look at her, but kept his eyes

on the rough floorboards, still unfinished. A work in progress—just like him.

"We'll have to work at it. Hard. We'll have to be prepared to give in sometimes. We can't run away when times get tough. We've got to keep working through the problems. That's how families are made. It's the rough times that make you solid, seal the bonds."

New life surged through his brain. Was she offering to help him? He waited, his heart racing a hundred miles an hour. Moments later her warm, dainty hand crept inside his.

"There aren't any guarantees with marriage, Gabe. I can't promise that it will always be sunshine or that you'll like everything that happens. I can't make the past all better."

"I know." He held her fingers fast, drawing air into his starved lungs as he listened to her words, heard the tentativeness in her voice.

"But I can promise that I'll stay here. I promise that I won't give up and run away. If you really want this, I'll do my best to make it work."

He fingered the ring on her finger, twirled it, caught a beam of light in it and let it play over the wood. And all the while he tried to control the emotion that made him want to bawl like a baby.

"I really want this, Blair." He forced himself to meet her steady regard. "I promise that I won't take off, won't fly into a tantrum, won't demand my own way all the time. I'll stick it out until you tell me to go. I'll be the best father and husband I can possibly be." He gulped down the fear. "There's just one thing."

She smiled that goofy, lopsided smile. "With you there always is. Well?"

"Don't expect perfection. I have no idea how things are supposed to work. I know diddly about family life and even less about being a father. If I'm doing it wrong, promise you'll tell me."

"Oh, I'll tell you." She smirked at him, then her face grew serious. "There's no 'supposed to' about this, Gabe. We make up our own rules as we go along. Nobody has all the answers except God, and if we trust in Him and keep pushing, we'll figure it out together. Okay?"

"Very okay." He slipped an arm around her waist and hugged her close, swallowing when she hugged him back in that free, generous, nondemanding way her family had. "Can I kiss you?" The words slipped out before he had time to think about the inadvisability of asking such a thing.

Gabe stared at her perfectly sculpted face and wondered when this need had begun to grow inside. He wanted to hold her close, to protect her, to keep her safe. But mostly he just wanted to hold her.

"I guess." She shrugged at his startled look. "Nothing has gone the way I expected lately. Everything seems bigger than life."

"Is this a bad time to tell you that there's going to be a hot tub at the end of the pool?" Gabe held his breath. To his amazement, she burst out laughing.

"Always full of surprises." She cocked her head, then slipped her arms around his shoulders. "If you're kissing me, you'd better get started. I hear the pitter-patter of Daniel's feet."

Gabe leaned forward and kissed her. As kisses went, it wasn't a ten. For one thing, he almost missed her lips. For another, he felt choked up with emotions of all kinds, and he didn't want her to guess that her words had touched him so deeply.

But the beginning of the kiss didn't matter. When his lips touched hers, it was perfect, right. He knew she was everything he'd wanted in his life, beauty, joy and a zest for the future. Maybe with Blair he could finally find some measure of peace.

"They're kissin' again," Daniel chirped from the doorway, making it sound as if his parents did little else.

Which, as far as Gabe was concerned, wasn't a bad idea at all. Not half bad.

Three weeks later, Blair sat in the upper balcony of the little church she'd grown up in and listened as the organist practiced for the Sunday service. There was no one around, no one to take her mind off her thoughts. No reason to mask the guilt.

You don't trust Gabriel Sloan. You don't need him—not really. You don't believe he's going to stick around. Why act as if you do?

Her conscience kept asking the same questions over and over.

Why pretend you've forgiven him when you know perfectly well that you're still nursing a grudge?

Blair sighed, the old anger at his cavalier treatment of her youthful innocence welling up anew. She shifted uncomfortably, remembering those moments at the castle when he'd opened up to her just the tiniest bit. He'd done that because he thought she trusted him. And she didn't. Not as she should trust the man she was marrying in a few weeks.

"Is everything okay, honey?" Aunt Willie slipped

in beside her and lifted one hand to brush away the tear that had fallen to Blair's cheek. "I know you think my pills make it so I don't see and hear a lot of what goes on, and maybe I don't. But can't you tell me why you're crying? I promise I'll try to understand."

"It's so hard, Willie." When Blair dashed a hand across her eyes she caught the flash of Gabe's diamond. The tears wouldn't stop. "He's done nothing wrong, nothing. He's really trying. He goes to Grandpa for advice, he's never angry or pushy with Daniel, he's really attempting to work through our problems."

"We're talking about Gabriel, of course?" Her aunt nodded her graying head. "And yet you still can't forgive him, can you?"

"It hurts, Willie. It really hurts. I loved him so much. I'd poured myself into that relationship, and he just threw it away. Now he walks back into my life and expects to pick up the threads. How can I do that? How can I just let it all go and say, 'Okay, Gabe, we'll be married. No problem. Let bygones be bygones'? I can't stop asking why. Why wasn't my love enough for him? Why did he need the protection of his money?" The words wouldn't stop. "Why did God let me go through that?"

"Because you needed to learn a lesson? Maybe to help you grow strong and rely on Him." Willie stared at the picture of Christ in the garden that hung above the choir section. "Honey, you know that Grandpa and I think the world of you, that we love you more than life, don't you?" She waited for Blair's nod. "And I would never purposely choose to hurt you, unless it was for your own good."

Blair made a face. "Uh-oh."

"You know what I mean." Willie leaned back and closed her eyes. "You're one of those people who need to feel useful, who need to *do*. You know I'm right."

"Yes, you are. But there's nothing wrong with that. Somebody's got to do things." Blair rushed to defend herself.

"Of course they do, dear. I'm not saying it's bad. I'm just wondering if perhaps, well, you get so busy *doing* that you're starting to believe your works are what make you strong. I've seen you almost run yourself ragged these past few weeks, hurrying here and there, trying to keep so busy you won't have time to think."

"I guess I don't know what you're saying." Blair watched the sun flicker across the stained glass windows, highlighting scenes from Jesus's life. "You think I should just sit and do nothing?"

"I think you should lean on God instead of your own strength. I don't know what's changed in Gabe's life. I don't know why he suddenly feels he has to start over, begin a new life. Maybe we'll never know. But I believe this is an opportunity for you."

Blair frowned, twiddling one curl around her finger as she studied her aunt. "An opportunity to do what?"

"To get past the past. To believe that God has forgiven that sin and that He doesn't see it anymore. He's already done it, but you're acting as if you can't accept His gift of grace."

"I am?" Blair considered the words while privately acknowledging the sting they brought to her heart. So even Willie had seen her bitterness.

"Aren't you? Isn't that what this taking care of everybody is about? You're trying to make yourself worthy of love, and you already are worthy. God loves you just the way you are."

"But I get so mad at him. Why wasn't he like this before? Why wasn't I smarter? Oh, I mess up so much!" The tears welled as the secret grudge inside her shifted until it was under the microscope of her heart.

"Sweetheart, we all mess up. Me more than most. You think you should be perfect and you want to know why God doesn't make you more like Him." Willie waited until Blair nodded. "He is, my darling. Every day. He's just not finished yet. But until He is, His grace is sufficient to overcome all of your flaws."

"But I'm not worthy of loving. I know He died for my sins, but I just keep on sinning. I get angry at Gabe when he tries to fit into our lives, when he assumes that we can be a family just because he wants it. How can I be a child of God and still do that?"

"Because you're human. And because you won't give up on this belief that you can earn love. You can't earn love, my dear. I don't love you because of what you've done for me. I just love you. That's it. No strings attached." Willie picked up Blair's hands, touching the diamond as she spoke.

"Listen. When Jesus died, He knew what He was taking on. He saw the sins you would commit, now and in the future. He knew all of that. And He forgave you. He took your place. You're not a prisoner anymore. You can walk away from guilt, stop worrying about being worthwhile. He loves you as you are." Willie squeezed her hand hard. Her voice dropped.

"The problem is, you don't want to extend that same grace to Gabe."

The words hit hard, scoring a direct blow on the bubbling cauldron of anger and retaliation that gurgled inside Blair's heart, begging release. She sighed, kicking her toe against the carpet.

"I want to believe that Gabe is sincere, Willie. I want to believe that he thinks more of Daniel and me than his company. I want to believe that I can rely on him. But I just can't. The past *isn't* past! It's right here beside me every day, every time I see him."

"Then let it go. Trust that God is in control and that He will work all things together for good. Give Gabe your trust." Willie's eyes fixed on her steadily, holding her gaze.

"How?" Blair mumbled, trying to look away but not succeeding. "How am I supposed to do that?"

"You know how, Blair. Deep in your heart, you know. Let go of the grudge. It's eating at you, ruining your joy. You can't change the past. You can't make it better. You only have now." Willie's fingers were gentle on her shoulder. "If you can't trust Gabe, you can trust God. Leave Gabe to Him."

It was hard to even think about what Willie, in her own quiet way, was suggesting.

"You want me to offer to sign the prenuptial agreement he had drawn up before, don't you? You think it will prove something to him." Blair crossed her arms and sprawled back on the pew. "You want me to go into this marriage with nothing, no guarantees, no plans to protect my son?"

"Isn't that how you were prepared to go into it before?" Willie's bright eyes demanded an answer. "You said it was Gabe who wanted the guarantees.

That you just wanted to love him. Now you have that chance. Grab it with both hands and stop worrying about what could happen."

Blair reflected on the past weeks, how she'd tried to show Gabe how good she was, good at mothering, good at caring for her grandfather, good at caring for Albert when he needed it; and how bad he was for forcing her into this situation.

"Gabe's just as scared as you, but with more reason. I believe he's never known the love of a family, never been freely given anything. He thinks he has to buy in. That's why the money's so important. It's his ticket to love." Willie rose to her feet and snatched up her purse.

"I promised I'd meet a friend for coffee five minutes ago. I've got to go." She hugged Blair in a tight, throat-clogging hug that told her niece how much she cared. "I want you to be happy, honey. Go into this marriage giving something that costs you dearly. Help Gabe understand that love can't be bought or sold. And remember that, no matter what, Mac and I love you."

"Thank you, Auntie." Blair let her go with a watery smile. "Bye. Have a good visit. I'm going to sit here for a while."

Willie hurried away, and Blair listened to the stairs creak as her aunt bustled downstairs. When all was silent, she let herself dwell on the idea.

Sign the prenuptial when he hadn't even asked? Give up all of her rights, all of Daniel's to help him believe in her love?

"I don't think I can do it, God," she whispered brokenly. "He owes me that, at least. Is it so wrong to want a little bit of security for my son? Anyway, for all I know, he isn't going to ask me to do that again.''

The tears fell unchecked as she wrestled with it. Then her eyes caught sight of the scripture verse sprawled across the front of the church in bold, black letters.

My grace is sufficient for you.

Enough to forgive the times she'd ignored Gabe? Enough to forget the way he'd just let her leave seven years ago? Enough to cover her sarcastic, cutting retorts?

My grace is sufficient.

She could take it or leave it, believe what the Bible said or muddle things up trying to find her own answers. God had done His part. It didn't say His grace *was,* but *is* sufficient. For everything. All the time. If she didn't accept it, was that God's fault?

A line from the pastor's sermon rang around the room as if he'd just spoken it.

''How do you react upon learning that God would rather die than live without you? You can't earn that kind of love.''

Blair felt the tears pouring down her face and knew that she'd been trying too hard. She wasn't worthy of love. She never would be. But God loved her anyway. So did Mac and Willie and Daniel. It was time to accept that love and do something with it.

Heavy footsteps made the stairs to the balcony groan. Blair hurriedly dashed away her tears, but stayed where she was.

''Blair? Are you all right? Willie said you were up here thinking. Is it something I've done?'' Gabe stood at the end of the pew, his big body partially bent as he tried to stand under the sloping roof. One hand reached out and a finger brushed across her cheek. "You've been crying," he whispered in wonder.

"Just a little." She clasped his hand in hers and tugged. "Can you sit down for a minute, Gabe? I need to say something."

His face tightened, and little worry lines crisscrossed his forehead, but he sat, his fingers still cradled in hers.

"I have to say I'm sorry," she began. It felt good to let go of that tight ball of anger.

"You're sorry? For what?" He stared at her as if he didn't recognize her.

"For nursing a grudge against you all these years. For making things hard for you ever since you've come." She hung her head in shame. "For trying to embarrass you in front of Mac and Willie and Albert so that you'd be uncomfortable. For not telling you about Daniel." The last words oozed out on a whisper of regret. "I stole those years from you, and I had no right to do that."

He reared back, his eyes bubbling with emotion. "No right? You had every right! I'm the one who should be apologizing."

She smiled at his one-upmanship. "Just let me finish."

"Sorry." He stared at their entwined fingers. "Go ahead."

"I want what you do. I want Daniel to have a father and mother who care about him, who do everything they can to make his world happy." *Please, God, help me.*

"What are you really saying, Blair?" Hope glimmered in the depths of his emerald eyes. His fingers tensed on hers.

She couldn't do it—couldn't say the words that would tell him how much she needed him. Something, some tiny reminder of the past, yanked her from the precipice of truth. What if he laughed? What if he left? She temporized.

"I'm saying that I will try as hard as I can to make this marriage work. I don't know how things will work out, how we'll manage everything, but I'll do my best to make sure Daniel sees you in a positive light. I trust you, Gabe."

Sometime during her little speech his eyes had moved to her face. As she spoke they seemed to dim a little, flicker, then cloud over, as if he was disappointed in what she'd said.

"That's all I can hope for," he murmured, dropping her hands. He shoved his into his jacket pockets. "I won't abuse your trust, Blair. I promise I'll do the right thing this time."

He stood, staring at her. One hand reached out to touch her hair in a featherlight caress that sent a tiny shock to her heart. He seemed to want to say more, but couldn't find the words. She thought he would kiss her, but then that fraction of a second was gone. At last he spoke.

"Are you ready to go?"

She nodded, gathered her things and trailed him down the stairs. "I have to stop at the florist's to make sure everything's under control. Could you pick up Daniel, then meet me at the grocery store?"

"Of course." He stood in the foyer, staring at the sanctuary. "I never went to church regularly, you know. Only with you and because of you. I never thought I was the type who needed it."

Blair waited, breath suspended. He was going to

tell her something about himself, something important. She forced herself to stand perfectly still and wait.

"My mother died when I was five. I think my father must have loved her very much. But when God didn't cure her, he sort of turned on the church and everyone in it. Mom made sure I went to Sunday school every week, but my father didn't care if I never went. We started to move around a lot, and I didn't know how to get to the church, so I stopped going. By the time I was old enough to go on my own, I didn't see the need."

He'd said *my father*. Not *dad* or *my dad*. The rock solid steadiness of his voice and the rigid line of his jaw told Blair how much he'd kept to himself.

"I think he was upset that God hadn't taken me and left her."

Blair sucked in a breath of dismay at the horrible words, but she didn't interrupt. He needed to get this out. Somehow she sensed that this festering sore was best treated in the healing light of the present, just as she'd had to face her own hidden anger.

"I was never the kind of son he wanted, you see. I was lousy at his favorite game, basketball. I had no head for baseball statistics, and I was too gawky and introspective to be put on show. I liked books. He hated reading anything but the sports page. I was too curious. I messed things up, and he had to pay to get them fixed." His eyes were almost blank, staring at her as he related his past with detachment.

"What kind of things, Gabe?" She tried to draw him out.

"What? Oh, toasters, his calculator, the radio and television. He sent me to my room for a day for that."

Gabe smiled a cold, hard little smile that didn't reach the ice in his eyes. "He did me a favor by doing that. I spent those hours reading up on all kinds of stuff. I guess I was a little too old for my age."

Blair nodded. She knew from their discussions in the past that his IQ was very high. She could imagine how little that endeared him to a man who thought sports was the be-all and end-all.

"He said I needed to learn responsibility, that I'd been babied. I got a paper route and squirreled every dime away. Finally I had enough to get an old, used computer when I was in eighth grade. A teacher at school lent me some parts, and I built Fred."

"I didn't know that." Blair stared at him. "The same Fred you have now?"

He grinned, life surging into his eyes. "Well, not exactly the same Fred. I've changed almost everything inside him about a hundred times, but he's still Fred. He was my playmate, my best friend when we moved too often for me to have friends." He frowned at her. "I don't know how I got started on this. I was talking about Sunday school, wasn't I?"

She nodded, disappointed that he'd closed the door to his past.

"Anyway, last year I got caught behind a car accident. I had to wait until someone could come and tow my car and, since there was a church across the road, I decided to go in and listen to the singing. They had this choir...." He closed his eyes as if remembering that day.

"You always did love music," Blair murmured, loath to break into his happy thoughts.

"Yeah. Well, anyway, they had more than good music there. They had a speaker who made sense of the Bible and God. I finally understood what my mother had taught me all those years before. We got to be friends, Jake Prescott and I. He needed some tech support, and I offered to help.''

"He got the president of the company to fix his computer?" Blair blinked. "But you always hated that aspect, the one-on-one.''

"This wasn't like that. It was more like two pals. Jake would toss in a comment about a computer being like God with all His intricacies. I guess you had to be there.'' He shrugged, his cheeks flushing a dark red.

"Anyway, he got me thinking about how I was living my life. He made it sound as if I was as much a pleasure seeker as my dad. I hated that, so I started to rethink things. I came to the decision that I needed to make God the center of my life. I just wanted you to know that we're on the same wavelength. I'm not exactly the same as I was. I'm not pretending Christianity anymore, Blair. It's the real thing now.''

She looped her arm through his, giving it a squeeze. "Thank you for telling me that,'' she whispered as she choked back tears. "It's important to me to know that we're on the same team. I know Mac will be glad when I tell him.''

"I've already done that. Your beliefs echo his. I didn't want him to think I'd try to alter that.'' He looked at her searchingly, his thoughts masked from her. Only the tiny quaver in his voice gave away his uncertainty. "Do you really think we can make this marriage work?''

She wasn't sure at all. But Gabe needed her. She knew it. "If we go in determined to make it work and rely on God's help, I know we can manage.'' She held her breath when his arm slipped around her waist. "Gabe?"

"I think this is the perfect place to make that pledge," he whispered as his mouth moved nearer. "I promise I won't do anything to make you regret marrying me, Blair. You can trust me."

"I do," she whispered, just before his lips touched hers. Then she gave herself up to the gentle reassurance of his kiss, shoving away the niggling voice that prodded, *Do you?*

Really?

Chapter Six

Mₐy seventh, his wedding day. Gabe stared as Jake Prescott, his best man, fraternized with the assembled crowd of townspeople. He shook his head in disbelief.

"I thought Teal's Crossing had a population of five hundred," he whispered to Blair. Her light scent caught on the breeze and carried straight to his nostrils, teasing him with the delicate fragrance of flowers mixed with something spicy. He didn't know what it was, but he liked it.

"It does. But the community is more than the town. Does that bother you?" Blair stood in front of him posing for the picture, her head tilted back. She smiled, and her whole face glowed with the warmth of the sun. And maybe something else. Maybe—happiness?

He thought about it for a moment, then shook his head. "I couldn't care less how many people are here," he told her honestly. "I know they came to see what kind of an outsider you're marrying, what kind of a father Daniel's getting. They're your friends, they naturally want to check me out.''

He listened to the photographer's request, then twisted his arms around her waist, clasping them together under hers, which still held her bouquet. In a bold move, he bent his head and pressed a featherlight kiss to her shoulder. This was the first time he dared such an intimacy, only because he could pretend to her that the photographer was the reason.

''Thank you, Blair,'' he whispered, resting his chin against the tulle of her wedding veil. He was totally awed by the fact that this gorgeous woman was his wife. Their relationship wasn't exactly the way he wanted it. Underneath her assurances, he knew that she still mistrusted him, still checked to be sure he meant what he said. She still wouldn't let herself need him.

But it was changing. Little by little Blair was getting used to him in her life again.

''For what?'' A glossy tendril brushed against his forehead, teasing him.

''For marrying me. For helping me with Daniel. For everything.'' He felt a surge of something warm and protective well inside. It wasn't love, he knew that. But it was still a good feeling.

''You're welcome.'' The whisper barely carried on the breeze. ''Here he comes again.''

Gabe stayed exactly where he was as Daniel raced up to them, jerked to a stop and held out the cushion that had carried their wedding bands earlier that afternoon. He looked so cute in his little black tuxedo, vest and bow tie that Gabe couldn't stop his proud fatherly smile. It widened even more when Daniel spoke to him.

"Hey, Dad, can I get rid of this? I'm tired of hauling it around." He thrust the creamy satin cushion toward them, his dark eyes sparkling. "What do you think, Dad?"

Daniel took every opportunity to use the term *Dad,* often repeating it to himself before he fell asleep. It was as if he couldn't believe God had answered his prayer.

Gabe looked over Blair's shoulder at the little boy, and suddenly he knew exactly how Daniel felt. The truth dawned like a white-hot light searing his brain. This, right here, was everything he'd ever wanted. He was part of it. He felt a tender but fierce protectiveness surge through him. His arms tightened fractionally around Blair's waist.

So he couldn't feel love, so what? He'd give everything he had to make this work. He had to believe that it would be enough for Blair and for Daniel.

"Sure you can, son. Give the cushion to Mac. He'll put it away till your mom has time to look after it." Gabe reached out and tousled the stick-straight hair, then grinned as Daniel jerked away.

"How come you don't have these pretty curls like your mother?" he asked, fingering one delicate strand as it lay against Blair's neck. When she shifted just a bit, he let his arms fall away but kept her hand wrapped in his.

"That's girl hair!" Daniel's voice oozed disgust. "You 'n' me are boys, Dad. We got boy hair."

"You sure are." Blair wiggled her hand out of Gabe's, then reached down and straightened the bow tie. She smiled when it immediately tipped to the right. "Your father has the same problem as you." She turned to face Gabe, her fingers plucking at his tie. "But just the same, you're both very good-looking."

He caught her fingers and held on, the whirring and snap of the camera a faint buzz in the background.

"We're not good-lookin'," Daniel said, obviously disgusted by that assessment. "We're han'some. Aren't we, Dad?"

"You're very handsome, son," Gabe answered, tongue in cheek.

"Girls are good-looking, Mom. Not guys. Right, Dad?"

Daniel's scathing voice drew Gabe's attention from Blair. Which was probably a good thing. He had a feeling he'd been staring at his wife again. Lately he couldn't seem to stop. She fascinated him. Her delicate but strong fingers, her tiny, efficient body, her quick brain.

"Hey, are we gonna get a girl for our family?"

Gabe straightened, his attention divided between Daniel and Blair as he considered the request. It was true, Blair didn't immediately tell the boy no, but it was also apparent that she was uncomfortable with the question. He'd have to step in.

Gabe let go of her hand and knelt in front of this precious child, swiping back a hank of Daniel's hair as he did.

"Nobody can know the future, son. We don't know what's going to happen. We just know that today is the first day for us to be a family. Let's enjoy that, okay?"

"Okay." Daniel grinned his half toothless smile and then raced away. He hurried back for just a moment. "I'm going to play with Joey Lancaster." In a whirl of black he was gone, his muddy shoes testament to his lack of concern for the rented suit.

"Joey Lancaster?" Gabe got to his feet, his eyes searching Blair's. "Isn't he the kid Daniel didn't like?"

"Was." She walked beside him over the lush green grass and toward the church. "They're best buds now that Daniel has a father, too." The photographer stopped them beneath a late-blossoming apple tree.

"Oh." Gabe digested that for a moment, amazed at the changes that had come into all their lives. He ignored the camera, though he heard it whirring madly behind them.

"I like your dress. It suits you." He fingered the delicate silk petals sewn over her shoulder, tracing a line to her waist. "It looks simple, but even I can see that it's really quite complex. And very delicate." His fingers traced the ethereal silk chiffon. "It's like you."

"I'm not that complex. Not really." Blair shook her head, curls bouncing. "And I'm not delicate at all. I'm pretty tough. But thank you."

"Are you glad Willie insisted on a traditional wedding?" He grinned at her fingers squeezing the bouquet he'd flown in. "Complete with orange blossoms."

She rolled her eyes. "That was your idea. All I wanted was to be married in a church by a minister with my family nearby." She glanced at the branch hanging over them. "And now it's apple blossoms."

He joined in her laughter, content to share the joy of the moment.

"Everything else about this wedding sort of mushroomed. Mostly because of Willie. She's wanted to do this for ages. I just couldn't stop her.''

Gabe glanced to where the older woman stood talking to a group of women, who craned their necks in his direction every so often. Great-Aunt Willie was clearly bragging about her nephew-in-law. He felt a surge of pride suffuse his heart.

''Well, boy. You did it!'' Mac bustled toward them, his leathery face wreathed in smiles. ''You're glad I sold you that land now, aren't you, son?''

''Yes, sir,'' Gabe agreed softly, his eyes on his wife. ''I'm very glad.''

Blair was immediately claimed by Clarissa and Briony, her attendants. They seemed eager to discuss the origins of her dress. Since Gabe knew very few of the locals and even less about wedding dresses, he walked away from the crowd, anxious to snag a few minutes on his own. He shoved his hand into his pocket and felt the sheaf of papers his lawyer had sent for Blair to sign.

Somehow, in all the fuss and confusion, Gabe had forgotten to ask her if she'd sign them.

No, he reminded himself, that wasn't true. He hadn't asked her because he hadn't wanted to remember the past, hadn't wanted to go through it all again. Hadn't wanted to tint this perfect day with the ugly memory of another wedding day.

Gabe let his mind go back to that morning in his penthouse seven long, empty years ago. He remembered the way the incandescent shimmer of joy had drained out of Blair's eyes as she'd read the papers he asked her to sign. He remembered how she'd carefully set down the pen, pressed the thick wad of legal papers on top of it and walked away from him toward the door.

"You don't trust me, Gabe." The hurt on her face still got to him. "You think that by signing that prenuptial agreement I will somehow prove to you that I'm not out to get you, that I won't ever hurt you." She'd shaken her head, that glorious hair tumbling around her shoulders. When she spoke again her husky voice was cracked and broken.

"I can't promise that, my darling. I probably will hurt you. Oh, I won't mean to. But one day I'll do something that will really cut deep and then you'll start to wonder if I'm just pretending, if I'm really after your company or your money. That's what it's all about, Gabriel, isn't it? Your precious money?" One small hand dashed away the tears that dimmed her telltale eyes. "You love your money more than me."

He'd denied it, of course. Tried to reason with her, to tell her that he cared for her. But Blair was adamant, and just as stubborn as he. She would not accept his argument that he was only following legal advice.

"I don't care a fig about your money," she'd insisted. "But nothing I can do is ever going to prove that. You have to trust me, Gabe. You have to take me as I am and believe that I want only the best for you. I won't go into this marriage with a way out already in place, with the steps to divorce already outlined. I won't start off expecting to fail. When I get married, it will be for life, to the one person who feels about me as I do about him."

She'd waited for him to say something then, but Gabe had no words. The fear was like a big cannonball lodged in the depths of his stomach. What if she was like all the others in his life? What if it was all an act, a way to get what she really wanted—not him, but his money? He'd have nothing again. He would have reverted to that sniveling little boy who had always disappointed his father.

"You have to start this marriage with faith, Gabe. That's the only way I'll ever be your wife. Think about it. I'll be waiting. If I don't hear from you, the wedding is off."

Well, he'd started this one with faith, though his lawyer would go crazy when he found out. He was taking a risk, of course. Blair might end up cleaning him out, taking everything he'd worked so hard to achieve.

Gabe shook his head. The idea was preposterous. She hadn't allowed him to pay for any part of the wedding.

"The bride's family pays for the wedding," she'd insisted.

Gabe let a tiny smile curve his mouth. Willie had proven a valuable ally. She'd been his eyes and ears, as well as a worthwhile asset, ensuring Blair wasn't forced to do without anything she wanted. He'd have to remember to thank her. Privately, of course.

Gabe perched on a rock by the creek, his finger rubbing against the band she'd placed there just a half hour before.

"The best man wants to know if the groom finally got cold feet." Jake's laughing voice penetrated his thoughts as his big, beefy arm thunked Gabe on the shoulder. "It's a bit late now."

"No cold feet, buddy. This is the first right thing I've done in a long time." Gabe waited while Jake found a rock to land his bulky body on. "You know I've been praying for an answer, and then God sent me here, thanks to Mac."

"'All things work together,'" Jake reminded him with a grin. "I must say she's a beauty. And that kid of yours is a real heart-tugger. You're going to have to be on your toes to live up to all that admiration."

"Don't I know it." Gabe felt the fear snake up his spine. "I haven't got a clue how to do that."

"Who does?" Jake shrugged. "Most men learn as they go, though they usually start with a baby and work their way up."

Gabe felt the heat singe his face. He grimaced. "Don't remind me," he muttered. "I know all about my sins."

Jake burst out laughing. "If God can forgive, I think you can, don't you?" He waited a moment, then reminded Gabe, "And if He's on your side, the battle's already won."

"It's just that I'm afraid Daniel will wake up one morning and realize that I'm as big a phony as my old man."

Jake frowned. "I don't know what you mean. You're nothing like him. I've seen you with Daniel, don't forget."

Gabe swallowed. "You know my problem, buddy. I'm not the type of guy who needs people. In fact, I function better without them. Nobody gets disappointed that way."

"How do you know? Ever stick around long enough to find out?" Jake shook his head at Gabe. "I know, I know. You think you're not capable of love. That it's not in you. That it got killed or something when you were a kid." He snorted. "That's a bunch of hooey."

"A bunch of what?" Gabe blinked at the vehemence in his friend's voice.

"Hooey. Malarkey. Garbage, pal. Pure and simple. God doesn't make people like robots or computer chips. He makes them with a heart and soul. Your heart isn't dead or frozen or any of those other things you keep thinking." The assurance in Jake's voice rang pure and clear.

"God is your real Father, Gabriel. He's not going to let you miss out on one of the best experiences a human can have. Just relax, enjoy your new family one day at a time. The time will come when you'll wake up and realize that somehow, some way, love got rooted inside of you and it won't let you go. You'll realize that the only person you want by your side for the rest of your life is Blair. Every moment you spend with her will seem like a miracle." He grinned at Gabe's surprise.

"What do you know about it, Jake?" he demanded, pessimism niggling into his brain.

"A pastor learns these things." Jake winked. "Sometimes it pops up in front of you so quick it knocks you off your feet, and sometimes it takes a while to push through the hard rocky soil. It'll come. Just have faith in God's leading."

"Easy for you to say." Gabe eyed him suspiciously. "Anything you want to confess, buddy? Somebody special knocked you off your feet?"

Jake ignored the question. "You can't control love, Gabriel. God's in control, and things work best when you don't apply for His job."

"Who is it?" Gabe leaned forward, intent on

guessing. "The pianist? Marion something?" He chuckled at the glimmer of light in the other man's eyes. "I knew you two had something going."

"We do not have something going." Jake glared, his cheeks bright red. "She tolerates me. That's about it. And we're not talking about me, we're talking about you."

"I'm a flop in the people department." Gabe sighed. "Yesterday I made Daniel cry. The day before that Blair nearly decked me. I don't understand what makes them tick. Why didn't God send me a robot? That I could understand, or tear apart until I did?"

Jake burst out laughing. "Life's not nearly as much fun with a robot, Gabe. What did you do, anyway?"

"To Blair?" He shook his head, held his palms up. "I have no clue. I thought I was helping when I told her she should have finished her degree. She's barely scraping by making the candles and honey, and she won't expand because she doesn't want to take on debt. She was holding a pail of honey at the time. I'm lucky I didn't get to wear it, judging by the look on her face." He yanked a despairing hand through his newly short hair. "How am I supposed to help her when I always say the wrong thing?"

"Idiot!" Jake backed off when Gabe glared at him. "Okay, sorry. But think about the past for a minute. She was pregnant—you were no help. What choice did she have but to quit school and go home to have her baby?"

"But after? You have no idea, Jake! She's a fantastic teacher. She made chemistry so much fun when I saw her teach. She's a natural." When he remembered the lights going on in those brains all those years ago, Gabe couldn't believe she'd walked away from it all.

Jake clapped a hand on his shoulder. "You've got to imagine yourself in her position. Okay, she had the baby. Now she's got to feed him and herself and take care of her kin. She's no doubt still upset, with herself and with you. But worse, she hasn't got any money to go to school, Gabe. She probably even had a few debts, scholarships notwithstanding. You're talking as if she didn't want to go back, when it must have torn her apart to drop out so close to the end."

Gabe shook his head, misery clogging his throat. "Money," he whispered. "It always comes back to money."

"No, it doesn't," Blair interjected as she reappeared. She stood behind Jake, her eyes soft as they met Gabe's. "I wanted to watch Daniel grow, to be there for him. I chose that above college. Someday I'll finish, but it's not a priority."

Jake bounded up from his stone and hugged her, completely disregarding the delicate fabric of her wedding dress. "You're my kind of woman." He chuckled. "Someone who doesn't care about the cash a fellow has. We preachers never seem to have two cents to rub together."

Gabe couldn't say a word. He'd never told Jake about the prenup agreement. He wouldn't now. He only asked himself why Jake was able to so clearly see into Blair's heart when he hadn't.

"Hey, Blair, want to know the most important thing to learn in chemistry?"

She grinned at Jake, her head wagging back and forth in admonishment. "Listen, sonny, I learned that the first day of my first year. *Never lick the spoon.*"

She giggled at his downcast look. "Now I've got one for you. How is the world like a beehive?"

Jake frowned. "I don't know anything about bees," he muttered. "It's an unfair question."

"Poor baby! Then I'll give you the answer. We all enter by the same door but live in different cells." She burst into tinkling laughter at his disgruntled look.

"There are some who think that anyone who makes a joke like that should be locked in their cell." Jake's dancing eyes made light of the threat as he hugged her again.

Gabe knew it was time to step in. "May I remind you that this is *my* wife you're hugging? Go after Marion what's-her-name if you need someone to hug." He wrapped his arm possessively around Blair's shoulders. "I can do my own hugging, thank you."

Jake's face grew serious. "I know you can," he murmured softly. "It's nice to see you realize that." Turning to Blair, he bowed gallantly. "I'm leaving you with him, but if you need help, just scream. I'll be glad to dunk him."

"You couldn't," Blair told him, her lips curving in a smile as she glanced at the stream. "It only comes up to his knees."

"Guess I'd have to shorten his legs, then." With that smart rejoinder, Jake ambled across the lawn to talk to Mac.

"I like your friend." Blair turned in the circle of Gabe's arms and met his steady gaze. "He's nice."

"He likes you, too." Gabe studied her beautiful face, accented with just enough makeup to highlight her big brown eyes. Today they seemed even larger and more shimmery. "I'm sorry I said those things about your degree, Blair. Clearly I wasn't thinking straight. It must have been very difficult to manage with a new baby and no income." He felt a stab of regret, but stuffed it away. He couldn't change the past, but he had now. And maybe, God willing, the future.

"It was difficult," she murmured, her hands moving to straighten his cummerbund. "But I'll choose family over anything else every day of the week. That's just the way I am."

"I know." He drew her into his arms and rested his chin on the top of her head. "I thank God for that every time I look at Daniel. You've done a wonderful job with him."

He felt her take a breath.

"Thank you. I had good material."

"I'll try not to mess up, Blair." To his surprise, she pulled back a few inches. Her eyes were darker than ever, her cheeks blazing.

"Will you stop saying that! You're his father, you'll make the decisions you think are proper for him. So will I. I trust you with him, Gabe."

But you don't trust me with you. You think I'll hurt you again.

Gabe brushed his lips against her forehead, then drew her back where she belonged. "Thank you," he whispered, his eyes closed tight as he accepted the tiny crumb of faith she'd just placed in him. It was a start.

They stayed like that for several minutes, the peace of the valley landscape surrounding them, the chattering voices only a few feet away drowned out by the gurgling brook and the babble of birds and squirrels.

"Gabe?" Blair's voice was so soft he almost missed it.

"Yes?"

"Do you think you could kiss me, like a man kisses his new wife, I mean?"

Gabe's eyes flew open in stunned surprise at her hesitant request. At that precise instant he realized their son was about to interrupt. Again.

He tipped her chin up so he could get a good look into her eyes. What he saw there made his stomach quiver.

"I could and I will." He memorized each detail as he spoke, ensuring that she heard what he wasn't saying. "But I'd rather do it when we're alone and can't be interrupted by—"

"Dad! Mom! Come on, Mac says it's time to eat."

Blair shrugged out of the lovely wedding dress and carefully hung it in its protective cover inside the massive cedar-lined closet of her new home. She slipped into her swimsuit, then pulled on her old favorites, a flannel shirt and soft, worn blue jeans. If Gabe wasn't around, she intended to try out that pool.

Seconds later, her sandals clicked against the tile as she slipped out the patio door of the master suite. She paused in the fragrant rose garden and drank in its beauty. Overhead, a blanket of stars twinkled at her in friendly silence.

"How did he do it?" she marveled, walking around the perfectly planned garden.

"Sheer brute force. And threats. Lots of threats," Gabe said, coming up behind her in the garden. "I don't take no for an answer. Plus, most of it has been planned for a while." His hands on her shoulders gently eased her to face him.

"I hope it didn't embarrass you that the men I hired to transport everything put all your things in there. I thought we'd split the suite. I've been sleeping in the dressing room. I'll stay there."

She nodded, having already suspected this was his plan. Gabe was a proud man. He wouldn't want anyone speculating on his private life. "Is Daniel asleep?"

"Totally conked out. He was in the middle of asking me another question when his mouth drooped and he was out of it." Gabe laughed softly. "He's quite a kid."

"He certainly loves this place." Blair grinned. "And why not? How many kids do you know who have their own private pool, not to mention that playground. He's going to spend tomorrow racing back and forth from one to the other. You'll have to teach him to swim."

Gabe's hands dropped away from her arms. The jerk of his body, the sudden chilly silence made her frown. What was wrong now?

"Gabe? What is it?"

"You'll have to teach him. I can't." Ice shivered through the words.

"But I meant when you learn. I wasn't…all right." Blair wouldn't argue. But something was wrong here. "Is there some reason you don't want to teach him?" she asked carefully.

"A pretty good one, actually." His mocking voice told her how upset he was. "I can't swim."

She vaguely recalled his past words. "Yes, I know.

You were going to teach yourself. But, then, why such a big pool? A status symbol?'' That explained it. Only the best for Gabe Sloan.

"No!'' He exploded, his face contorted into a mask of fury. "I couldn't care less about symbols.'' He stomped down the path toward the stream that ran behind the garden, his shoulders hunched defensively.

Blair waited a few minutes, then followed him. This wasn't what she'd expected, but she'd promised to be there in good times or bad. Tonight was clearly the latter.

"Gabe?'' She found him on the little white bridge that gave a view of the waterfall in the distance. Someone had installed a floodlight, and the sight was breathtaking. Blair decided to check it out another night. She faced him. "Please tell me what's wrong. I'll help if I can.''

He snorted, but his voice sounded less harsh. "You can't help. No one can. It's in the past, but I can't let it go.'' When she didn't say anything, he turned to her, fury darkening his eyes to emerald chips. "I thought I could prove that I was more than what he said, that I didn't botch everything. I thought, Blair swims. She even likes it. I can do that. I'll get a pool and I'll learn to swim. I'll swim in it every day. That'll prove I'm not a wimp, a loser.''

Blair almost laughed at his words, then realized he was deathly serious. This was a situation that needed defusing. Now.

"A wimp?'' She made herself laugh. "You? How ridiculous! Clearly whoever said that didn't know you at all.''

The words seemed to draw him out of his rage,

calm him. He turned to her with a question in his eyes.

"Well, think about it. There aren't too many wimps who build a company out of nothing, take on the competitor and buy them out, let their father fleece them out of hundreds of thousands of dollars and still come out on top." She rolled her eyes at his frown. "I read about it. So sue me." She veered back to the subject of this contretemps. "Something is wrong with your picture, Gabe."

She stood beside him in the night, oblivious to the croaking frogs all around them, hearing nothing except the tortured note in his voice.

"How does your not being able to swim fit into this picture, Gabe?" She leaned her elbows on the rail and cupped her chin in her palms while she waited for him to open up. How had she never suspected he had such scars? Why had she never seen them buried under his quiet dignity?

Because you weren't looking for his good side. You only wanted to see his faults.

"I'm not leaving until you tell me," she informed him when long minutes passed without any words.

"Sometimes you are so...bossy. Stay out of it, Blair."

His teeth were clenched. She could see his hand fisting on the wood right next to hers. And suddenly she realized that this wasn't just about the past, it affected the present, too.

"I'm not out of it. I'm married to you. We have a son. This concerns all of us. I want to know why it's so important to be able to swim."

"No." His foot scraped across the wood, signaling that he intended to leave.

"Yes." She stood erect, facing him in the gloomy light. "We're in this together. No secrets, no lies. No pretending. Just honesty. That is what you said today, isn't it?"

He huffed and puffed, but finally sighed his agreement. "Some day you're going to have to learn to back off."

She nodded. "Okay. Some day I will. But not tonight." She took his hand and led him to a patio chair near the pool. "Sit down and tell me what's wrong."

Blair held her breath. Gabe sat, but his mouth tightened to a grim, thin line. His fingers bit deeply into the cushions of the chair. His face grew tortured.

"I'm scared of the water." The words burst out of him like a dam spilling a lake held too long in abeyance. "I'm a chicken, a coward. I can't stand the thought of it closing over my head." His eyes blazed into hers. "So you see, he was right. I am a wimp."

"Wait a minute. Who is *he?*" There was no point in backing off. She knew that instinctively.

"My father." The cold hate in those words cast a chill on the lovely evening.

"And how did he manage to equate being afraid of water with a person's worth? Doesn't that seem a little skewed to you?"

Gabe's head jerked up, his brows joined in a frown. "What?"

"I mean it. The guy obviously has problems or he wouldn't have stolen from you. But since when do you measure yourself against that kind of standard?"

"Since I panic every time I get near the stuff."

Blair tried to pray as she listened, tried to ask for heavenly direction to this very earthly problem. She knew there was something more, something he wasn't saying. Gabe hadn't explained why he was afraid of water. But right now, that didn't matter.

"And you don't want Daniel to see you panicked, is that it?"

His head jerked once in an affirmative.

"Go get your bathing suit on, Gabe."

"What?" He stared at her in worried disbelief.

Blair stayed calm. "Look, you've let this rule you for far too long. Fears can be overcome. Everyone has them. It's time to get working on yours." She undid her shirt and slipped off her jeans until she was standing in her swimsuit. "I'll teach you how to swim, Gabe. Go get your suit on."

Some of the tension eased, though his shoulders stayed taut. "You'd do that?"

"Why not? You built this monstrosity. Seems a shame not to get some joy out of it."

His voice barely broke the quiet of the evening. "I was going to force myself, you see. That's why the pool was included in the plans. I was going to acclimatize myself to it, teach myself to take it one step at a time."

"Only you couldn't do it. Of course you couldn't, not by yourself. I'll help you. I love swimming." She sat on the chair. "Go get your suit," she said patiently.

He took his own sweet time, but finally Gabe emerged on the patio in a pair of dark blue swimming trunks.

"I switched on the lights," he told her, his voice losing some of its innate authority as he stared at the glassy-smooth water.

"I saw." Blair got up and walked to the pool's steps. She waited, holding out one hand. "Come on.

Let's go in. It's a beautiful night for a swim. Look at those stars.''

He didn't look up, he just stared at her. Finally, with effort, he managed to put one foot in front of the other and walk slowly to her side.

"I hate this," he muttered, his eyes blazing as he stepped into the water.

"I love it." She kept walking steadily forward, letting the water slide up her body. "It makes me think of God's love, covering me like a second skin, protecting me."

Gabe searched her eyes, waiting as she walked him deeper into the water. When the water came up to his shoulders, he stopped. "That's enough." His voice was hoarse.

"Okay." She led him back a little way, wincing as she flexed her tightly held fingers. "Gabriel, you are in control here. If you want your head to go under, it will. If you don't want it to, it won't. It's your choice. No one is going to force you."

Blair dipped under the water, then slowly stood, letting it stream down off her head and face. Gabriel stared at her, then, before she could react, dipped himself completely under the water. He came up thrashing wildly, his eyes full of terror, coughing the water from his lungs.

Blair waited until he'd recovered, then smiled. "You have to close your mouth," she whispered tenderly. "You're not going to drown. I won't let you. It's only water. It can't hurt you."

He didn't look convinced.

"Try again," she encouraged. "But this time take a deep breath and don't let it out until your head is out of the water."

"This is stupid." He turned as if to leave.

"What's stupid is letting fear rule your life. It only makes everything worse." She made no attempt to stop him.

When he got to the steps Gabe halted, then turned back. "It's been there a long time," he told her quietly. "It won't die easily."

"You wouldn't be suffering so much if it were easy." She stood silent, waiting.

Gabe returned, but his mouth was set in a grim line. He gasped a huge breath, ducked his head under and popped up a nanosecond later. "There," he spluttered.

"There what? Are you over the fear? Can you swim here with Daniel now?" She waited.

Gabe muttered something then resolutely forced his head under the water several more times. Each time Blair watched but said nothing.

"When will it be enough for you?" he asked angrily after the last attempt. "I can get my head under. I can stand it. Isn't that enough?"

She shook her head. "While you're under there, your mind screams to get out. You can't swim when you feel like that. You have to relax in the water." Blair took his hand and led him toward the steps. "Sit down here. On this step." When he was up to his neck in water she sat on the step above. "How does it feel?"

"Wet." He let go of the railing long enough to wave a hand through the pattern of light that shone from the bottom. "I should have put in more lights."

"Why? Is there something hiding in the corner? Some monster that will jump out and drown us?" He glared at her in silent anger, but Blair wouldn't give up. "The monsters are here, Gabe." She tapped his head. "It's time to toss them out."

It took a long time, and she was beginning to wish she'd never started this, but finally Gabe sighed.

"All right!" His eyes met hers. "I wasn't much older than Daniel. We'd gone to the lake one weekend. He pushed me out of the boat in the middle of the lake and ordered me to swim to shore. 'Any little wimp can swim, you know.' I had no idea how to stay afloat. I grabbed onto the rope from the anchor but that infuriated him. He grabbed my head and shoved me under. I must have blacked out because the next thing I remember is waking up cold and wet on the shore. He was nowhere around."

The shockingly brutal words stripped away her pretense at nonchalance. Blair could only stare at him in grim commiseration.

"Now you know the truth. Are you happy?"

The biting sarcasm washed off her. He was hurting. And she hurt for him.

"Are you?" she asked softly. "It wasn't the water's fault, Gabe. It was his. Think of it like this—the water is like wings. It buoys us up, lets us travel in ways we never could have without it. It was given to us for our enjoyment. It's one of God's good gifts." She slid one arm along his shoulders. "Lean back against my arm and look up at the sky."

Hesitantly, slowly, Gabe let himself lean back, one hand clinging to the handrail.

"See those stars," she whispered. "They look like thousands of diamonds strewn across God's black velvet cloak. If you keep your eyes on the ground you miss them."

She held him there for a long time, supporting his

head, softly reminding him of all the glories God has provided for his children. When Gabe finally stood, she waited, wondering how far this could go.

Her heart ached for the poor little boy, denied worth by his own father. How could she resent him? How could she add to the misery and suffering he carried still?

"I've had enough. You can swim your lengths if you want. I'll sit here and watch."

Blair nodded and struck out for the deep end, sliding into a smooth, regular front crawl that stretched her muscles and soothed her mind. She'd missed this. The university pool was an extravagance she no longer had when she'd moved home. To be able to swim at night, in the open air, seemed decadent beyond belief.

When at last she could find no more breath, Blair stroked over to the steps and sat beside Gabe, letting the lapping water ease the sting in her chest.

"How did you learn to swim?" Gabe asked.

"Grandpa Mac. My parents died in a boating accident, but he was determined that it wouldn't deprive me of the joy of water. I was about five when he first brought me to the creek. It was freezing cold but he made it all a game. I loved it."

Silence, yawning and cavernous, accentuating the different histories, hung between them. Blair finally got up.

"Good night, Gabe."

His hand on her arm stopped her. He towered over her in the gloom, his eyes glowing. "Thank you," he murmured.

Blair nodded, her smile sincere. "Thank you for the pool. I love it."

She made it to the patio door before his voice stopped her.

"Blair?"

"Yes?" She turned slowly, watched him climb the stairs, pad across the cement.

"I promised you earlier that I'd kiss you when there was plenty of time and no one around to interrupt." He waved a hand. "There's no one else here."

Blair glanced over her shoulder, then nodded. "That's true. They've all gone to bed. First night in their new home. I don't think they'll miss the old place, but we'll leave it there in case one of us needs a hideaway."

"And I've plenty of time."

"So do I." She wouldn't back away, not now. This was not the Gabe she'd known. This man had pushed away her defenses and climbed right into her heart. Whether he knew it or not, he needed her. She wanted him to kiss her.

He stepped forward until there were only millimeters separating them. One hand lifted to cup her chin while the other wrapped itself around her waist. His eyes stared into hers, asking a question. She stared back, hoping he'd understand her answer.

His lips brushed hers in the gentlest of touches before they moved to graze against the tip of her nose and over her eyelashes. They caressed each cheek, then followed the line of her chin to her mouth.

When he finally moved away, he muttered, "It's a good thing nobody saw that. I've been wanting to kiss you for a long time, Blair."

"Me, too," she whispered, before turning tail and dashing into the house to the security of her bathroom where the knowledge glared at her in the mirror, lit by the bright white lights behind her.

She loved Gabriel Sloan, far beyond the silly schoolgirl infatuation she'd thought was true love back then. The emotion burning deep inside now consumed her. It was pain and pleasure. He didn't love her, but that didn't matter. She wanted only his happiness, his freedom from the fiendish memories that haunted him.

She would help him as much as she could, no matter what it cost her. And maybe someday, Gabe would see that he needed her, too.

Someday.

Blair walked into the massive, empty bedroom and sighed.

What a way to spend your wedding night—alone.

Again.

Chapter Seven

"Daddy? Can I help?"

A week after the wedding, Gabe glanced up from the complicated diagram, sparing a glance for the little boy before his attention was lured by the intricate work. "Uh, not right now, okay, Daniel? I've just got a little extra touch-up to do here, and I'll have rebuilt that microprocessor." He studied it more closely, checking and rechecking the alterations he'd made on the diagram.

"What's a micropro—that thing?"

"It sorts through the information. Kind of like the brain." Gabe checked to make sure, but Daniel still stood by his knee, his hands at his side. "Why don't you go play with your blocks for a little while?"

"I want you to come, Daddy. You know how to build it better than me."

"In a minute." Gabe took a second look at his solder. Yes, that would hold. Now if he had thought this through properly... He turned back to the papers.

"I'll hold it, Daddy."

The shrill sound drew Gabe out of his introspection in time to see one small, chubby hand reaching up to touch the circuit board Gabe had just assembled.

"Don't touch that!" Gabe grabbed for the board, but instead of hanging onto it, his fingers slipped and the assembly crashed to the floor, sending shards of electrical parts all over. Four days of work—gone. "Daniel!"

The boy backed away slowly, his eyes huge in his white face. "I'm sorry. I didn't mean to do it. I just wanted to help. I'm sorry."

"Sorry isn't going to put it back together again, Daniel." Gabe fought to control his frustration. Evidently he took too long because Daniel turned and fled, his little feet pounding up the stairs to the main floor.

Furious at the mess and the time and effort lost, Gabe went looking for the broom and dustpan. He found them and Mac in the kitchen.

"What's biting your ankles? You look like a thundercloud about to dump on someone." Mac sat in his favorite chair, tipping back on it so he could stare at Gabe. "Having some trouble?"

"I wasn't until Daniel knocked an assembly onto the floor." He pinched his lips together, frustration vying with anger, neither of which he intended to let out.

"Was the boy hurt?"

The comment struck Gabe to the quick. The dustpan fell from his suddenly nerveless fingers. "I don't think so," he muttered, feeling the heat of shame burn his face.

"Didn't you check?"

It was a question, that was all. There was no condemnation in Mac's voice. But Gabe felt the guilt all the way to his heart. "He ran away so fast I didn't get a chance." It wasn't an excuse, and Gabe knew it.

He let the broom hit the floor and flopped into the chair opposite Mac's.

"I blew it. Again." He raked a hand through his hair, his shoulders slumping in defeat. "I just got so involved in what I was doing. I forgot he wouldn't understand how delicate everything is. I didn't mean to yell. I just wanted to warn him. Now he'll think I hate him or something." Gabe sighed, then got up to pour himself a cup of coffee.

Mac held out his mug. "He's probably feeling bad, all right," he agreed quietly.

Gabe's stomach plummeted to his shoes.

"But that's not necessarily a negative. Next time he might think first and ask permission before he touches something." Mac took his full cup, sipped it and then sighed his satisfaction.

"But I shouldn't have yelled at him. He's just a little kid. He wasn't trying to steal a company secret." Gabe wished he could wipe it out and start again. "Now he'll hate me. I'm doing exactly what my father did."

"Are you?" Mac swiveled his toothpick to the corner of his mouth, his lips smiling. "I don't think so. Parents are people, too, Gabe. They make mistakes. They yell when they shouldn't. Life happens. There's nothing wrong with a child learning that everyone makes mistakes. It's how we handle them that matters."

Gabe stared at him. "I don't think I know what you mean." He managed to squeak the words out, studying the older man's relaxed posture. "You mean you're condoning my mistakes?"

"I mean you walk up those stairs to his room, where the boy is probably sniffing his head off, and you tell him that you're sorry you yelled, that you still love him and that he needs to ask permission to touch your stuff."

A sudden picture floated through Gabe's mind. He'd been, what, six? His father had blown his top when a cup, one of his mother's special ones, slipped from his hand and smashed on the floor. He hadn't meant to drop it. He just wanted to touch it, remind himself of her. Now, years later, he could understand that his father had resented the shattering of her belongings in the same way he'd hated losing the woman he loved so desperately. But at the time, at six years old, Gabe had only understood that he was a clumsy, stupid nuisance.

"I should have known better." He swallowed the strong black coffee without thinking, then winced as the bitterness burned down his throat.

"Do you think you might be expecting too much of yourself? You're not perfect. Apologize and move on." Mac drank the thick black stuff as if it were water. "I've gotta get moving. I'm going fishing."

Gabe watched him amble across the room, the heel of his hand massaging his thigh as he went. "Can it be that easy?" he wondered aloud.

"What?" Blair breezed in through the patio door and poured herself a glass of lemonade from the fridge. "Oh, that's good! I never did say thank-you for the housekeeper. I don't know how we'd manage this place if you hadn't hired her to keep things going." She wiped a hand across her forehead, took another swallow, then flopped on a chair. "Can what be that easy?" she repeated.

Gabe studied her upswept hair, the damp tendrils curling against her neck, her dusty white shirt and worn jeans. She glowed with good health. Did she ever make mistakes?

"Gabe?"

Slowly, he related the incident in his workroom. "I guess I forget he's only five—almost six," he amended with a halfhearted smile.

"And he should know better." She pushed her glass away, plunked her elbows on the table and leaned forward, cupping her chin in her hands. "He wants a father, Gabe. Not an angel."

"I don't think we have to worry there." Gabe pulled his handkerchief out of his pocket and wiped the dirt off her nose. "You're supposed to leave the garden outside."

She grinned. "Dirt's good for the skin. Some people even use mud packs." Her hand closed around his. "He won't hate you, Gabriel. He'll think it through and understand if you explain."

Gabe let her hold onto his hand. It felt good, reassuring. "I'm so lousy at this!" He glared out the window at the burgeoning blooms that seemed to tumble everywhere, out of old pots, a one-handled wheelbarrow, a rusty watering can. "I sounded exactly like my old man."

"He was a father, too," she reminded Gabe softly.

Gabe's head jerked around as he stared at her.

"You can't keep on hating him, Gabe. It'll only eat you alive. You're you. You have your own chance to deal with your child the way you believe is right.

Daniel knows you don't hate him. Talk to him. You'll see.''

''Will you come?'' He held her hand a little tighter, knowing somehow that if Blair was there, everything would be all right.

''I don't think so.'' She eased her fingers away from his, but one hand lifted to brush his hair off his forehead. ''You and Daniel need time together on your own. You're walking on eggshells around him. Therefore he's not sure what to expect. Just be yourself, Gabe. Relax. He's only five.''

''That's what scares me,'' he muttered, knotting his hands together.

Blair leaned over and brushed a kiss against his cheek. ''Be strong, big guy,'' she teased, her voice brimming with something he thought was gentle mockery. Then she got up, bunched her hair under a ratty old sun hat and grinned. ''Back to the petunias.'' She giggled. ''I ordered way too many.''

''Maybe you should put hives around the yard. With all those flowers, the bees would really work.'' He was only joking, but Blair didn't know it. Her forehead furrowed as she considered his idea.

''It might work,'' she muttered to herself, pushing the door open. ''And I've got those hives repaired now. I could...'' She left talking to herself.

''Daddy?''

Gabe twisted in his seat. Daniel stood in the doorway, tearstains on his cheeks, his feet shuffling nervously.

''I'm sorry. I didn't mean to wreck your microphone thing.'' A big shiny tear slid down his cheek. ''I'm sorry.''

Gabe's heart ached for the uncertainty in those

eyes. He'd done that—him, the guy who should know better. "Come here, Daniel."

Daniel took one faltering step forward, but that was enough for Gabe. He scooped him up in his arms and set him on his knee, one arm around his shoulders.

"First of all, it's called a microprocessor. Can you say that?" He waited until Daniel had faithfully repeated the word. "And secondly, you don't have to apologize. I should be doing that. I didn't mean to yell at you. I never wanted to do that. I'm very sorry for it."

"That's okay." Daniel patted his cheek, his eyes bright once more. "I yell when I get mad sometimes. It makes me feel better."

"Well, it doesn't make me feel better. I just feel sad."

He hadn't meant to say it, but with that silky soft hair beneath his chin and the cuddly little body settled on his knee, Gabe was beyond controlling his words. "I don't ever want to scare you or hurt you, Daniel. But I'm not very good at being a daddy and sometimes I might. Will you remind me if I do it again?"

Daniel cocked his head, his eyes searching Gabe's. "I guess." One hand reached up to touch the furrow between his father's eyebrows. "Are you mad now, Daddy? Do you want me to kiss it better?"

All of the angst, the tension, the frustration slipped away as Gabe stared into his son's earnest face. He nodded, his throat too choked to speak. When the pudgy arms slid upward to circle his neck, when the soft little mouth brushed over his cheek, Gabe wanted to cry.

Thank You for this wonderful gift. I don't deserve

it. This special little boy is far more than I ever dreamed of. Please, don't let me mess up.

"Is it all better now?" Daniel's worried voice broke into his thoughts.

Gabe slid his arms around that wriggling little body and hugged for all he was worth. "Thank you, Daniel," he whispered, as he breathed in the half-dust, half-soap scent of his very own child. "Thank you very much."

"Welcome." Daniel hugged him, then giggled. "Your chin scratches me. Can we go help Mommy now? I love planting flowers."

"Sure we can. Then maybe she'd like to go down to the creek and cool off." Gabe let the boy drag him to his feet and lead him to the door. "What do you think?"

"She likes the pool better." Daniel scurried down the path. His voice echoed on the warm spring breeze. "An' I like ice cream. Chocolate ice cream, with marshmallows and nuts."

"Everything okay now?" Mac sat on the patio, whittling something out of a piece of willow. "Got it all straightened out?"

Gabe nodded, unwilling to speak for fear Mac would hear the emotion that still gripped him.

"Thought so. Kids don't hold grudges, Gabe. It's adults that do that. That's why we have the heart attacks and ulcers. The kids have shed all that and moved on. We hang on and let the bitterness fester so bad it affects everything we do. Lesson there somewhere, don't you think?" Mac winked at him, then went on carving and whittling, whistling an old western tune as he worked.

Thus ignored, Gabe set off down the flagstone path

to the gazebo Blair was intent on surrounding with flowers.

Was that what he'd done—let his anger and frustration about the past affect his whole life? Was that why things had looked so bleak after his father had swindled that money? It wasn't because he needed it, Gabe admitted wryly. He could give away three times that much and still fare quite well.

It was the loss of trust that bugged him. His own father had manipulated him into feeling guilty because he'd wanted an ordinary father-son relationship.

Why was that so wrong?

Because you're never going to have it. Face up to the facts, boy. You're not the kind of son he expected or wanted. Now move on.

Gabe wanted to forget it all, he really did. But the hole inside yawned deeper than ever, reminding him that he had no father now. He'd cut him out of his life just like he'd cut out everyone who tried to use him. He was Gabriel Sloan. He didn't *need* anybody.

Up ahead he could see Blair, face glowing with joy as she perched on her hands and knees, digging in the dirt. She didn't have to do it. He'd told her he could hire someone. But she'd insisted. And there beside her, his hands copying his mother's movement, kneeled Gabe's son.

What would happen if he lost them both? Why did even the thought of it fill him with terror?

Chapter Eight

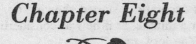

Blair packed the crate with candles and carefully set it on the floor. Automatically her hands reached for another box and she began assembling an order.

Time flew so fast these days. It was hard to believe she'd been married two weeks, that Gabe's castle had been finished well before the deadline and they'd all moved in together.

So little had changed in her life, and yet everything was different. For one thing, she had too much work.

"Can I help?" Gabe stood in the doorway of her workroom, tall and uncompromising.

"If you want. I'm filling orders." She shrugged, unnerved by his sudden appearance. "Aren't you busy with something?"

He and Albert had been closeted for days, building some gizmo that remained top secret to everyone but them. She had to give Gabe credit, however. The moment Daniel came home from school, he put everything on hold to spend time with him.

"Not right now. We've hit a jam." He took the

list she handed him and began selecting items. "Do you have a lot to ship?"

"Quite a few items. Then I've got to get moving on the Christmas stock. That's my biggest season, and everything has to be at the stores by the first of October."

He nodded. "I know. In L.A. last year they hadn't even taken Halloween stuff off the shelves before the Christmas decorations started showing up." He studied her for a minute, as if he was considering his next words. "You look tired."

She rolled her eyes. "Thank you, Gabe. That's nice to hear."

"I meant it more as a question than a complaint," he said mildly. "You're doing too much. Can't you ease off a bit, let someone else do some of these jobs you've taken on?"

Blair felt a little burn start deep inside. "There isn't anyone else. Do you think I'd be doing that fundraising if someone else had volunteered? Besides, I like to be busy."

He shook his head in patent disbelief. "This goes way beyond busy, Blair, and you know it. You used to do this before."

"Before what?" She recounted her order and realized she'd put in too many flared red candles. When Gabe didn't say anything, she stopped what she was doing and looked up. "Before what?" she repeated, annoyed that he was interrupting.

"In L.A., when you were running from one thing to the other. Maybe that's why I never knew much about your family. You were always dashing from one place to the next."

"You weren't exactly sitting still yourself," she

reminded him bluntly. "I'm not the one who canceled out every other night because I had to work."

He nodded. "I know. I did a lot of things wrong in those days. But we're talking about you. Who are you racing for now, Blair?"

She sighed, raked a hand through her mussed-up hair and spared a moment to glare at him. "Nobody. Myself. I don't know what you're saying." She threw up her hands in disgust. "There are things to be done, Gabe. I do them. No big deal."

He stared at her for a moment, then walked over, reached out and lifted her hand and, without really trying, slid her rings off her finger and then back on.

"You're losing weight, Blair. You never relax. You're tense all the time. When Willie's up half the night with her nerves, so are you. When the neighbors need a sitter, you rush over. When the school calls about drivers for the field trip, you volunteer, even though it isn't your son's class." He wouldn't let her hand go. "What's wrong?"

"Oh, for goodness sake!" She yanked her hand away and flounced to the coffeepot. "I like to be busy."

"This is frenetic." His voice held a hint of steel as he lifted the pot out of her hands. "You drink way too much of that stuff." He tossed it down the sink and switched off the machine. "Come on."

Blair was too surprised to stop him until he'd urged her out of her shop and into the yard. "Come where?" she spluttered when she finally found her voice.

"I don't know. For a walk." His hand held hers, not loosening a fraction when she tried to tug away.

"It's your day off, Blair. Time to get out of the mad rush and enjoy life."

She marched beside him, her temper rising. "This is rich, coming from the workaholic of the century!"

He ignored her sniping and led her around the side of the house. "I found a wonderful path behind here. There's the loveliest little spot on the top of the hill that overlooks our valley."

Blair sighed. "Gabe, I've lived here for years. I know all the sights."

He stopped and stared at her. "Do you? Really?"

She didn't know how to respond to that so she stayed silent. After a moment he resumed walking, tugging her along like a recalcitrant child. Only then did she notice the backpack swinging from his other hand.

"What's in that?"

He glanced over his shoulder, followed her stare to the pack and grinned. "Lunch, al fresco. Sloan style."

"All right, I'm coming. You don't have to drag me, you know." She pulled her hand away and forced herself to walk on, even though his pace made her lungs burn. Why was she so tired?

"Where's your energy now, Blair?"

She looked up. Gabriel stood atop a rolling hill, his hair whipping in the wind, his handsome face perfectly lit by the sun. While she watched he flopped on the ground, stretched out on his back and gazed into the blue sky.

Blair forced herself the last few torturous steps, then collapsed beside him, barely noticing the hardness of the ground as she gasped for breath.

"Remember when we used to go for walks?"

His voice seemed far away, and Blair turned her head to check. Gabe's eyes were closed, his hands crossed behind his head. He looked perfectly content.

"I wondered why you always headed for the beach. I used to think it was the water, but it wasn't, was it? It was the wind." His eyes opened, their clear green startling her with their intensity. "You felt free with it blowing away all the worries."

She shifted so he couldn't see her face.

"You don't have to hide. Willie told me a little."

Blair jerked around. "A little what?"

"A little of your past. That you've always been the responsible one, always protected those you love. It must have been hard to leave them here while you went to school."

"Yes, it was." She wished he'd get off the subject.

"Why didn't you tell me more about them? All I ever knew were their names. 'Grandpa and my great-aunt,' you called them. I can't remember one time when you really talked about them." His hand tilted her chin so she had to look at him. "Why was that, Blair?" He lay on his side, arm tilted so it supported his head.

"I don't know. I guess it just never came up."

"It should have." His fingers played with her hair, twirling the ringlets, then letting them fall against her cheek. "Were you ashamed of them?"

"No!" She jerked upward. "How could I possibly be ashamed of the people who took me in and raised me with nothing but love? No." She shook her head adamantly.

"Then why?" He seemed to ponder the idea for only a moment before his fingers closed around hers where they lay on the grass, fiddling with a stem.

At his touch, Blair froze.

"It was me, wasn't it? You were ashamed of me. You knew they wouldn't approve of me in your life."

The words pinged softly into her brain, tearing open the truth. "It wasn't shame." He had to know that, to understand. "I loved you then."

"But?" Gabe was sitting beside her. His hand wrapped around hers and squeezed in encouragement. "It's all right, Blair. You can tell the truth."

"I wasn't sure of you. I wasn't sure you knew who I really was." She blurted a stream of hurt. "All you ever saw was this person in glamorous clothes, pretending she fit in with the in crowd. You didn't know the real me, not even when you saw me at school. You thought my degree was just a hobby, didn't you? Something for me to do in the meantime?"

He considered it. "No," he said as he stared out over the valley. "I don't think I ever thought that. You were too good at what you did." His head reared up, his eyes bored into hers. "But you're right, I didn't know you. Not the real you. I thought you liked the fancy clothes, the parties, the glitz. I didn't realize that they meant nothing. I guess I'm only beginning to understand that material things have never really mattered to you."

"I do like the castle, Gabe. You did a wonderful job. I appreciate all the little things you incorporated to make it comfortable for Willie and Mac and Albert." She let the truth ring through her voice. "Not to mention Daniel."

He nodded, his face serious. "That's exactly what I mean. For *yourself*, you couldn't care less. It's your family you're concerned about. I'm just beginning to understand how much they mean to you."

"My family means everything to me." Suddenly she realized that Gabe was part of her family, too. She could see by the twinkle in his eye that he'd hit on the same idea.

"Even me?"

"Well, of course, you're i-important," she stammered. "I mean, I owe you a great deal."

"You don't owe me anything, Blair. Even in this day and age a man expects to provide a home for his wife and child." He shrugged carelessly.

"And her grandfather, her aunt and a man who's no relation at all?" She kept her gaze steady on him. "That's a great deal for anyone to do, Gabe. Let alone someone who's not..." She let the words die away, unwilling to finish.

"Someone who's not in love?" he asked. He shook her hand off his arm. "I do not want you to feel obligated to me. You do *not* owe me, Blair. Do you hear me? I will not be added to the list of people you have to repay!" He surged to his feet in one lithe move and stood glaring at her. "That's not what I want from you."

Blair sat where she was and studied him. This was the Gabe she remembered, strong, in control. His eyes sparkled, and his hands were planted firmly on his hips, daring her to contradict him.

This was the man she'd fallen in love with.

"Well?" He glared at her. "Don't just sit there. I want your word that I'm not going to have to hear you thanking me for every rock and stone of our home. I did it for me, too, you know," he grumbled, his chin thrust out. "I like Mac and Willie. I needed somebody like Albert to keep me on my toes. He's got more ideas than I do."

She burst out laughing, good humor restored. "All right, Gabe. I'll only say it this once. Thank you very much for accepting my family as yours and for giving us such a lovely place to live." She grabbed his hand and pulled herself up, standing on tiptoes to press a kiss against his lips. "Thank you. For the last time."

Before she could move away, his arms came around her waist and his mouth landed on hers. When he finally lifted his head, Blair opened her eyes and blinked twice, only then realizing that her arms were around his neck, her fingers embedded in his hair. She pulled them away and shifted until his arm was loosely around her waist.

"If you say thank-you one more time," he warned, his eyes glinting with suppressed emotion, "I'm going to kiss you again."

"Hmm." She pretended to think about that.

He laughed, hugged her close, then let one arm drop away to snag the backpack. The other he moved to her shoulders, holding her at his side as they walked across the hill.

"Can I ask you something, Blair?"

The uncertainty of the question made her wonder, but she decided to face it head-on and whispered a tiny prayer for help.

"Go for it."

They walked for several minutes before he finally allowed himself to ask, "Why didn't you tell me about Daniel? Didn't you think about it, wonder if I'd want to know? Were you so afraid I'd take him?"

Blair took a deep breath. "Yes," she whispered, and saw his chest sink as he took the hit. But she had to tell all of the truth. "And no."

"What does that mean?"

"I realized that I didn't want Daniel growing up in your world." She took a deep fortifying breath and let the truth spill out.

"I became someone else there, Gabe. I wasn't me, I was someone who was playing me. You were right. The only time I could really breathe, really feel free, was when I was on the beach. It's hard to pretend on a beach."

"It is?" He frowned, considering.

"It sure is. The wind messes your perfect hair, the sun melts your makeup, the sand gets in your clothes. And the water washes away everything but the basics." She stopped and faced him. "I was living a lie, even though I didn't realize it. By the time Daniel was born, I'd begun to look past the mistakes and see the root problem."

"Which was?" Anger was in his voice.

Blair sighed. "The root problem with me is that I don't fit in in L.A. At first I didn't think I fit in here, either, but it's like buying shoes."

Gabe blinked and knocked his fist against the side of his head as confusion clouded his eyes. "I wonder if I'll ever be able to follow your thinking. What do you mean? Your logic escapes me."

"Just listen. Sometimes I buy shoes that fit like a glove. I hardly notice I'm wearing them. Call them sneakers." She waved a hand. "This place is like my sneakers."

"Okay." He waited patiently, one eyebrow tilted up.

"For me, L.A.—your style—was like a pair of very high heels. Okay for a little while, but eventually you have to take them off or your feet get very sore and messed up."

"Okay to visit but you wouldn't want to live there." He pondered that. "What you mean is that you didn't dare tell me about Daniel because you couldn't imagine me living anywhere else?"

She nodded. "I never dreamed you'd come here. You always seemed intent on frequenting the in places, hobnobbing with the big boys."

He snorted. "Hardly hobnobbing, Blair. I doubt they ever even noticed I was there."

She smiled. "It was the place you wanted to be. I just couldn't see how Daniel would fit into that, even *if* you'd changed your mind."

Sorrow vied with wry reluctance on his face. "That remark will haunt me forever, I'm afraid. I freely admit it, I was a fool. Daniel is a godsend. I'm glad I have a son." He pulled her to a stop. "I'm hungry. Can we eat lunch here? It's so pretty."

Here was a lovely grassy spot beside the creek where it tumbled over rocks. Blair nodded and within minutes Gabe had spread a blanket and laid out some plastic dishes, two napkins and an odd assortment of food.

She watched, mouth pinched in a prim line as Gabe unpacked chips, peanut butter sandwiches, two sugar-free lollipops, a piece of leftover pie, six grapes—rather the worse for wear—and a thermos of—

"Water?" she squeaked.

"Water. You need to lay off that stuff you call coffee. Last night your hand was shaking when you were dipping those candles. It was probably from exhaustion, but all that caffeine doesn't help."

Blair tried to chew her peanut butter sandwich as she considered this. Finally she swallowed. She had to ask. "You're concerned about my health? You, the junk food addict?"

He was affronted. "I'll have you know that I've become very health conscious." He munched on a couple of grapes.

"You?" Blair could hardly imagine it. "The man who loves everything fried and nothing green? Amazing." She glanced at the pie. "Who's that for?"

"Half for you, half for me. I'm not totally reformed." He flashed her a smile that made her tummy clench and her toes tingle. "If you can't stand plain water, I brought along some lemon wedges. Let's see." He rooted through a bag and finally emerged with two plastic-wrapped halves, which he squeezed into her water.

"You've got more on you than in the glass." She sipped it, then forced her pursing lips to unclench. "Lovely." It wasn't easy to suppress the shudder at the sheer sourness of it. "You certainly have changed."

"Well, I'm trying." He took a sip of her water, made a face and handed it back. "That's too sour."

She burst out laughing. "Maybe we could dissolve the lollipops in it. Of course, we'd be putting that fake sugar chemical into our body. That can't be good."

He frowned. "I never thought of that. Hmm. Guess we'll have to make do with the chips. They're low salt."

"Then why bother?" Blair said grumpily, but she was hungry so she munched on a few of the flat, tasteless chips and the sandwich. Screwing up her courage, she finally asked the one thing that had preyed on her mind for weeks.

"Why did you decide to move, Gabe? Did something happen?"

He was silent a long time. Blair had decided he wasn't going to answer, that it was time to pack up and go home, when he spoke.

"I couldn't go on."

The harsh words hit her hard. "What do you mean?"

"It was gone. All the fun, all the thrill of making things work, the anticipation—it was all gone. I was stuck in a rut making decisions about stuff I didn't care about. I was so bogged down in details there was no time to do what I really liked. I knew if I didn't get out then, I never would. I'd be caught in the cycle of endless meetings."

Blair smiled, remembering his ability to submerge himself in his work without noticing time or people. "You always were a loner. You preferred the solitude of working by yourself. Even I knew that."

He nodded. "So did I." His face tightened. "I knew it but I couldn't accept it. You see, Blair, I figured it was something my father had inflicted on me, that it was antisocial behavior I'd developed from being alone too long." He shoved their lunch remains into the knapsack, shuffled over until he was beside her on the blanket, then picked up her hand.

"I figured I had a flaw, a weakness that needed fixing. The only way I could think of to fix it was to be in a crowd. Do you understand?"

"You mean you were proving something to yourself by hanging around those celebrities?" She couldn't quite see in-control Gabriel as that needy, but then, maybe she hadn't really known him.

"Exactly." He fiddled with her rings. "I hated it.

I wished we were somewhere else, just the two of us. Listening to the waves, maybe. Or at the library while you studied.'' He cleared his voice. ''After a while, I thought you were beginning to enjoy it. That really bothered me.''

''Enjoy that *circus?*'' Blair couldn't help it. She burst into laughter at the mess they'd made of everything. They'd been so stupid, so foolish.

''Do you know how many times I ate snails just because I thought you loved them?'' His lips turned down in distaste, and she laughed even harder. ''I hate snails—I don't care what they call them or how elite they are.''

''I do, too.''

''Anchovies?'' She waited for his nod. ''Caviar?''

He shuddered. ''Fish eggs? No, thanks!'' Suddenly he caught on. ''Screaming over music so loud your ears hurt? Having everyone call you 'darling' because they can't remember your name?''

She giggled at his pronunciation, then laughed even harder when he started on the vernacular she'd never understood. They laughed until their sides ached and they could laugh no longer.

Blair lay on the blanket, peering at the sky as she remembered those days and her fear of doing or saying the wrong thing, of asking to leave early and worrying that Gabe would miss out. After a few moments she turned her head toward him. Gabe was staring at her, his mouth twisted in a lopsided grin.

''You have my permission to shove my head under the water in the pool and hold it there for as long as you want.''

She giggled. ''You have my permission to demand

I wear four-inch heels for the next week without taking them off.''

He groaned, closing his eyes. "What a pair of fools! When I think of how many sinus pills I took after breathing that smoke, I could boot myself down the hill.''

"When I think of listening to Eunice blabber on about Pippi and Poppi, I could push you down it with no compunction.''

He shouted with laughter. "Those ridiculous dogs!'' he exclaimed. "How did you stand having them underfoot all the time?''

"Underfoot wasn't bad. It was in my bag that really got me. 'Pippi just adores tuna!''' She repeated the phrase in Eunice's shrill falsetto. "Maybe I owe those dogs. They helped me keep my figure when you kept feeding me those lavish meals.''

"Hey, I thought you liked Antonio's!'' He held out one hand with a flourish. "We have the chicken cordon bleu that madame loves as the special tonight.''

Blair held her aching stomach. "Yuck! I haven't eaten that since I left.''

Gabe studied her for a long time, his smile fading. "I'm sorry I put you through all that.''

"I'm sorry I pretended to be someone I'm not and made you think it, too.''

They looked at each other, awareness tingling between them. Blair was so conscious of Gabe sitting next to her, she could feel the hairs on her arm stand at attention. When he reached out to brush her bangs off her forehead, she leaned toward him, holding her breath as his fingers slid across her brow and over the curve of her cheek. They stopped at her jawbone.

"You're very beautiful,'' he whispered. "That

hasn't changed one bit. I used to be so jealous when you'd get into those discussions with your chemist friends. I had no idea what you were talking about, but I knew they were admiring you.''

"I hated the starlets fawning over you.'' She kept her eyes down. "I couldn't compare and I knew it.''

"Blair?'' He waited until she looked at him. "I only ever saw you.''

Tears pooled in her eyes at the wonderful compliment. "Thank you,'' she whispered, staring into that dear, solemn face.

A slow, provocative smile took possession of his face until his mouth was a wide white grin in his dark skin. "I told you, I don't want your thanks.''

Blair blinked. "What do you want?'' she asked warily.

His eyes dared her to listen. "Lots of things.''

"Like what?'' She couldn't turn away, couldn't get free of his magnetism. He drew her to him with a smile.

"Laughter,'' he murmured, his hand sliding down her back. "Lots and lots of laughter.'' His hand moved up, and moments later her hair tumbled around her shoulders. "Picnics.''

"Without lemons.'' She nodded. "What else?''

His hands cupped her face. "Time,'' he whispered. "Time to get to know you, to understand why you drive yourself so hard. Time to learn what you really like, what you want from life.'' He closed his eyes and thought for a moment. "Time to teach Daniel to ride a bike, time to learn how Mac knows so much. Time to help Albert perfect his gizmos. Time to go to church together, to sit all lined up in that pew like a real family.''

"Time to let go of the past and build a future." She waited for his response.

His words came on a rush. "Yes. I want that, Blair. I want to start over. I want to build something good, something we can be proud of."

"We've got lots of time," she murmured, her eyes closing as his thumb traced her lips. "All the time in the world."

"I hope so." He kissed her so gently, so tenderly, that the tears fell of their own accord. He wiped them away, helped her up and walked her back without saying a word.

As she stood in her workroom alone, Blair lifted a hand and traced her mouth, remembering. He was so sensitive, so considerate.

But will there ever be enough time for him to learn to love me, God? Will there be time and faith enough for that?

Chapter Nine

"Blair?"

"Yes?" She turned from the delicate task of rolling a sheet of beeswax into an intricate design she'd almost perfected. Gabe stood in the doorway, his face a comical expression of confusion as he studied the mess littering her workroom.

For the past three weeks, ever since the wedding, while busying herself with every job she could find, she'd secretly watched him. The old Gabe seemed to be back, at least the innate curiosity that had drawn her to him in the first place. But a different facet of his personality had also emerged. This Gabe seemed more determined, more purposeful. Which was all right as long as he didn't superimpose his will on hers.

"When is Daniel's birthday?"

Blair clapped a hand over her mouth as reality hit home. "Good grief, I almost forgot! It's Saturday." That glittering stare of his forced her to think a little longer. "Oh, no!" She closed her eyes and groaned.

"I promised to help out with the Scouts on that wiener roast."

"I know. Someone named Mona Greeley just phoned to remind you." Gabe glared at her. "How could you *forget* his birthday?"

"Don't look at me like that!" Anger simmered just beneath the surface. Gabriel Sloan dared to remind her of her own child's birth date? It was laughable. "I've been a little busy, you know."

He nodded. "A little too busy. I told you that a week ago. You can't keep this up, Blair. Daniel doesn't want Willie or Mac reading to him *every* night. Sure, they can pitch in once in a while, but it isn't fair to count on them all the time."

"I don't. It's just been very hectic." She gently squeezed the wax together with the rose imprinter. The simmering inside her inched up a notch to a boil. "They don't mind helping out, and it's good for Daniel, too." She reached for another sheet of wax before glancing at him. "It wouldn't hurt you to read to him. You're his father."

Gabe's jaw tightened. "I know that, thank you. I understand the ramifications of being his father, but I can't do it all. He wants you there, too. He wants you to hear all about his day and listen to his prayers. I've tried, but evidently I don't have the same method as you." Gabe yanked an old rickety chair forward and sank into it. "He keeps asking for you, Blair. Can't you put off your work for just a few minutes to spend time with your son?"

The pot inside her began to boil and bubble, roiling with indignation that edged nearer the top.

"That's rich, coming from you!" She set down the wax in case she damaged it with her taut fingers.

"I've spent six years of his life being everything to my son. I don't neglect him. I don't abuse him. I love him with all my heart. I spend as much quality time with him as I can. I certainly don't need lessons from you!"

His cheeks darkened. "I'm not suggesting you do. I know you love him. But he's confused right now. His whole world has changed, and he just wants his mommy to tuck him in. Is it so much to ask?" His voice rumbled low, condemnation in its depths.

Blair strove to remain calm as she clenched her hands together.

"I do tuck him in, as soon as I get back." She forced her fingers to unbend and started fiddling with the ribbon she wrapped each pair of candles in. She couldn't do anything because she was too angry, but she would put on a brave front.

Silence loomed between them. When Gabe finally spoke there was a hint of reprimand in his tone that scratched against her conscience like a fingernail on a blackboard.

"I thought we were going to make time for each other. To do things together." His hands reached out and stopped hers, holding them still between his palms. His eyes were mossy dark as they met hers. "When, Blair? When do we make time? You're always running."

With a pang, Blair realized she was so tired, she just wanted to cuddle in those arms, close her eyes and let him hold her. She wanted to forget about all the demands on her time, the challenges she'd taken on without thinking them through.

But the table between them was like the gulf that separated them. She loved him. He didn't love her.

She had to be strong, reliable, dependable. She couldn't need him. There was no telling where the next test would come from. She had to be ready.

"I'm doing my best, Gabriel." She tugged her hands out of his and moved to the box table, assembling the small white cardboard sets that had her name scripted across the top in gold lettering.

"No, Blair. You're not. You're letting your priorities get skewed." He grimaced, a wry smile on his mouth. "I should recognize the signs. I did it myself for enough years."

The simmering started again.

"Willie has never been better. She doesn't get overwhelmed by things nearly as often, and she hasn't asked me one of her goofy questions in days. Mac is as healthy as he's been in years. He loves working on that fountain you guys started. Albert's knee-deep in his inventions, and Daniel is finishing his first school year." She took a deep breath and glared at him. "Everything seems perfectly fine to me."

"Everyone is adapting to the changes we've made. Everyone except you. You haven't had time to figure out what's changed, what you need to change, because you're too busy running." He stepped around the table and stood beside her. His fingers reached out and plucked the cotton knit away from her rib cage. "This fit you perfectly a month ago. Now it bags and hangs. You've got blue lines under your eyes. Even when Willie sleeps, you don't."

"I'm sorry I woke you. You should close your door," she muttered stiffly, risking a glance in the mirror across the room. He was right, she did look awful. "I have a lot of things on my mind."

"Too many things. You need to get rid of some of them."

She frowned, disbelief fogging her brain. "What did you say?"

"I said it's time to cut down on some of this frenetic busyness. Today. Now." He refused to back down, though she gave him her fiercest glare. "I'll help you, Blair. However you want. But you've got to squelch this inane desire to run yourself ragged."

"I have a business to run!" She shouted it, tiredness and frustration lending an edge to her voice. "You may be able to hire a thousand minions to take over when you disappear for months at a time, but I can't."

He stared at her, his emerald eyes piercing. "Why not?"

She sighed. It wouldn't do any good to argue with him. And she didn't want upsets in the family. She wanted everything to run smoothly. She'd try reason.

"You don't understand."

"Try me."

Peacemaking got shoved to the back burner. "Look, Gabe. It's a complicated process that I developed myself. I take pride in what I sell, and I don't want that compromised."

"So you train someone to do it as well or better. Someone who will do this while you catch up on the important stuff like garnering new accounts, building your business." He waited, one ankle crossed over the other, his perfectly pressed jeans absolutely stain free. "I'll find someone for you if you like. I'll even design a brochure advertising your wares."

"You?" She scoffed at the absurdity of it. "What

do you know about making candles or producing honey?''

"Not a thing. But I do know that you need someone reliable, someone dependable who takes special care in their work." He reached out and pushed a curl off her face.

"I can't afford to hire anyone." She tilted away from his fingers, contrary to the ache in her heart.

"You can't afford not to. If you keep on like this, you'll get sick. The orders will back up, and nothing will sell. It's time for some strategic planning, Blair." He crossed his arms.

For some reason that motion made her burn. "I suppose you think, since you're the big tycoon, that you know all about this."

He chuckled. "I should. I've been through it enough times. Every little bit of growth, I'd have to revamp and revise. I wanted to do it all myself, but I just couldn't handle it. Rich had to practically force me to hire a business manager. He threatened to quit more times than I can count unless I followed the man's advice." He waited a minute, then lifted an eyebrow as if he knew the question that burned on the end of her tongue.

"The answer to your question is yes, I hated every minute of it. It hurt to let go and watch someone else take my ideas and run with them, even though it was my company they were building. I wanted them to be my designs, my work. In short, I wanted to control every minute detail."

"Sounds like you." She sniped at him because he'd just said the exact thoughts that had passed through her head. She hated the thought of relinquishing control. If she did it, she knew exactly what she'd get. Her standards would be met. If she let go…

His hands on her shoulders jerked her attention to him.

"It isn't easy to let someone else in, Blair, but it's the only way to grow."

Was he talking only about business?

"A company that's built on one person is no stronger than a family that is made up of one person. More heads, more shoulders, the idea pot gets richer. Besides…" He grinned and winked. "There are more shoulders to take the stress."

Were they stronger as a family now? Had moving into the castle with Gabe, giving Daniel two parents, had that made them stronger? Or had it weakened her?

"It takes a while, Blair. You have to give it a chance. That's all I'm asking. Let me find someone to help you out here. Someone who won't mind starting off at a lower salary if they can share in the benefits of making the business grow."

"Profit sharing." It was a good idea.

"Exactly." He grinned that big, flashy grin. "If you don't like what I find, we'll keep looking."

She felt foolish for not thinking of it sooner. "I suppose you think this is all rather silly," she muttered, waving a hand around the messy workroom.

He frowned, his head tilted. "Why would I think that?"

"Well, there's you and your company. What do you have now, Gabe, five hundred employees? Annual sales figures that fit right in with the Fortune five hundred fellows?" She laughed bitterly. "And you see me struggling with this little company that's liable to get eaten up by the giants. I suppose you think I should dump it all and be content to just be the little wife?'' She jerked her head, ready to take it on the chin.

His voice, when he finally spoke, was very quiet. ''You already are my wife. I don't see why that makes you any less capable as a businesswoman.'' His eyes held hers. ''I certainly don't blame you for wanting your own successful company. Why shouldn't you want to succeed, just like everyone else?''

A tiny hint of something—what, hurt?—echoed through his words.

''I've never been a snob, Blair. I don't look down on this business or any other. Why should I?'' He picked up a bottle of color. ''This shade of blue is new, isn't it?''

She nodded, pleased that he'd noticed.

''I imagine it took you hours of mixing and testing to get exactly this shade of greenish blue. You weren't satisfied until it did exactly what you wanted in the wax. I'm guessing that the technical part was fairly easy thanks to your chemistry background, but the trials, the run-throughs, the mistakes and retries, those must have been time-consuming, not to mention frustrating.''

She nodded again.

''But you persevered until you had distilled out of that exactly what you wanted. Why wouldn't I admire that?''

''I'm sorry.'' Shame burned on her cheeks. ''I shouldn't have said it.''

''I'm glad you did, because it brings home what I've been trying to say.'' He put the color down and turned to face her fully. "Our marriage is like that color. We need to test things out, make sure we're getting exactly what we want, and if we aren't we need to change the formula, rearrange the sequence, add more of one thing, take away something else."

"And you want me to cut down on work? How is that going to help?" She glanced at her watch, wondering if she'd manage to get anything worthwhile done today. The thought made her flinch.

Wasn't her marriage to Gabe worth some time?

"I don't want you to quit on your company, Blair. I think it's great. I'd like to help you with it, if you want me to. I'd just like to see you cut out some of the other extraneous stuff that takes time away, time that we should be spending with Daniel. And with each other."

The phone rang. Blair let the answering machine take it, her face burning as she listened to the teacher at the day care remind her that they didn't have much time to raise the last bit of money they needed. She glanced away from the machine as the message ended and caught Gabe's look of frustration.

"I'm sorry if you feel I'm neglecting you!" The words spilled out of her with a bitter ring, and she regretted them as soon as she'd said them.

Gabe's lips tightened. His hands balled at his sides. Then he turned and walked to the door, his voice hard and cold. "Forget it, Blair. Just forget it."

Tears welled in her eyes as she heard his truck door slam. She walked to the door and watched him drive away, her heart aching for the stoic look on his handsome face. The quiet, controlled rev of his engine, the steady hum as he drove out of the yard and toward his castle condemned her more clearly than anything else could have.

Why do I do this? Why do I have to prove myself? Is it ever going to be enough?

She flopped down on the doorstep and sighed.

Gabriel Sloan was right. And she knew it. She *had* taken on too much. The worst part was, she didn't know how to get out of all those commitments. Even as she'd thought about it once or twice, more had piled up.

It's just like our marriage. We need time to figure out what works.

Was that what she was afraid of—working out her marriage? Or was she afraid that it would never work out?

Blair closed her eyes and prayed.

Lord, I'm so tired and so confused. I want to do what's best for everyone and I just seem to be making matters worse. Please help me to find a way to reach Gabe.

The relief of admitting she was caught in a situation she couldn't control left her breathless. What to do now?

He wants to help, to be part of your lives. Let him.

Blair shuddered at the idea. Mind Your Own Beeswax was hers and hers alone. She'd started it herself, nurtured it until she had a firm client base with a regular order list. She didn't want to turn it over.

"You want to be in control."

The memory of those words made her blanch. It was true. She didn't want someone to tell her when and how to do things. She wanted to do it on her own. Just as she'd wanted complete control all those years ago.

You've been on your own. Look where you're at now.

Blair couldn't ignore the truth anymore. She sighed and got up. A quick check ensured there was nothing that couldn't wait. She snatched up her keys and locked the door, her mind in turmoil as she tried to think of a way to explain her sudden change of heart to her husband. Nothing but a bald admission of her mistakes came to mind.

She drove home trying to decide how to eat crow.

The perfect sunny afternoon sparkled off the shining windows of Gabe's castle from half a mile down the road. It shimmered in the blooming flowers that snuggled against the sidewalk and sparkled off the brook where it had been diverted to pass through Mac's newly created fountain.

Blair pulled her hair away from the nape of her neck and breathed in the heady fragrance of lilacs that wafted from a bush that had crouched against a huge glacial stone for as long as she could remember.

No one seemed to be around, so she wandered through the house to her room. The patio door stood open to the afternoon breeze. The glittering reflections of the pool beckoned her to dive in. It was an invitation she couldn't resist. Five minutes later she took a header into the water and let it course over her.

She burst to the top, feeling the water stream over her head and down the length of her hair like a cleansing tide.

"I thought you were working." Gabe lay sprawled on a lounger, clad in a white T-shirt and black swimming briefs. His black sunglasses effectively shielded his eyes from her.

"I decided I needed a break." She saw him glance at the phone he held. "Am I bothering you?"

"Of course not." He put the phone on the table. "Feels good, doesn't it?"

She glanced at him in surprise. "You were in?"

"I've been going in two or three times every day."

She waited.

"It's getting easier." He poured himself a glass of iced tea, then held up the pitcher in a question. At her nod, he poured a second glass. "I play silly games that Daniel taught me, like diving for a penny."

"I'm impressed." Blair climbed the stairs, took her glass and sat on the edge of the pool. "I wanted to ask you something, Gabe."

"Ask away." He stayed where he was.

Blair turned so she could see his face. "I wondered if you'd like to donate to the preschool."

He choked on his drink, his head jerking in her direction. Blair didn't like not being able to read his eyes so she got up, walked over and removed his glasses.

"In the amount of two hundred eighty-seven dollars and forty-three cents."

The beginnings of a smile tugged at the corner of his mouth. "You're sure it's not forty-four cents."

"Nope. Forty-three. With your contribution, the preschool will have the requisite one thousand dollars I promised to raise." She dragged a chair around so she was facing him and sitting in the sun. "It's tax deductible," she reminded him when he said nothing.

"Oh, well, if that's the case, sign me up." He studied her.

Blair leaned her head back and closed her eyes, allowing the penetrating warmth of those rays to pierce right through to her bones. How wonderful to just lie here. "Thank you."

"Can I ask *you* something, Blair?"

She shrugged. "My life is an open book."

"Hardly." He took another drink. "Why the day care? It's not as if Daniel's there."

"It's not really a day care. More a preschool. I was the president the year we founded it. I sort of feel obligated to see it prosper." She remembered the flurry of getting it off the ground and the feeling of overwhelming pride at the looks on the kids' faces that first day.

"How long ago was that?" Gabe's voice rumbled from somewhere deep within his chest.

It sounded like he was laughing at her, but she couldn't be bothered to check. Blair kept her eyes closed and concentrated on absorbing as many rays as she could. "Four years ago."

His chair squeaked a protest. A moment later one big hand covered her arm. "You felt obligated all this time? You didn't think maybe you'd done enough, that it might be time for someone else to pitch in?"

She did open her eyes then, and found his face mere inches from her own. "No," she breathed, almost silently. "I guess I didn't. I just saw a need and decided to do something about it."

"I see." He sat back. "Someone named Marty called about eight cakes you promised for next week."

Blair knew he wanted to say something else, so she forestalled him. "Yes. For the bake sale. It's a missions project that raises funds for Christmas gifts for children in an orphanage in some part of Russia." She opened one eye slowly and winced at the frown on his lips. "I was going to ask some of the other ladies to help me, but most people go on vacation around this time of the year."

"There's a bakery in the next town. Saunder's, I think it's called. I ordered ten cakes. To be delivered the day of the sale." His voice dared her to argue.

She didn't. "Thank you," she murmured. "I was wondering how I was going to manage that."

"Daniel's teacher called to say they have enough money for their field trip, the pastor has found a new recruit to head up the meals on wheels team and Mabel somebody will take your place escorting the Scouts on their trip this Saturday."

Blair sat up, her temper rising as she saw the complacent look on his face. "How dare you!"

"Somebody had to. Willie's driving herself frantic worrying about getting ready for the seniors' retreat. She doesn't want to ask you for help because you're so busy." He tilted his head back and closed his eyes.

"I like being busy." She glared at him, fuming because he couldn't even see the daggers she was tossing his way.

"You're too busy. It's time to let go of some of this. There are other people who'd like to help out, you know. They're just intimidated by you."

It was a horrible thing to say! As if she steamrollered everyone without considering anyone else's feelings. That wasn't her!

"Stop pretending you're asleep and listen to me." She waited until he opened one eye, then launched into her spiel. "I asked for help. No one offered. I've asked for help a number of times. No one ever offers. Somebody's got to do it."

"Maybe they just wanted to be asked. Personally. And left to do the job the way they see fit."

Something in the way he said it made Blair stop. She stared at him for a minute, turning over the words he'd just uttered. Suspicions crept through her brain.

"How did all these things just happen to come together today?" she asked softly as she swung her legs over the side of her chair and moved so she was mere inches from his face. "Exactly what have you done, Gabriel?"

"You always call me by my full name whenever you're ticked." He didn't bother to move back, just sat there studying her with that serious, intent look he gave to some of his biggest projects. "It reminds me of Miss Milton in third grade. She was a termagant."

"What did you do?" She prayed that he hadn't embarrassed her all over town by saying she was tired, haggard, needed help, was unable to cope. She didn't want that kind of attention or pity.

"Me?" He blinked innocently. "I just went for coffee to that little restaurant in town."

"Uh-huh. And my aunt Susan is a truck driver. Spill it."

"I didn't know you had another aunt."

She reached for the pitcher.

Gabe's gaze narrowed as he assessed her seriousness. Apparently he was convinced. "I went for coffee, Blair."

She picked it up and held it above his head.

"Honest!" Gabe held up both hands. "I may have mentioned that I wished my wife had a little more time at home, for me and our son. I can't remember now." He smiled like the wolf enticing Little Red

Riding Hood. "It was just guy stuff. You know, newlywed questions and all that."

Blair groaned. She could just imagine it. A bunch of the locals hearing that the groom was being ignored by the bride. Sympathy. Vows to help him out. Calls to their wives.

"My name will be mud." She set the pitcher down, walked to her chair and flopped into it. "I'll be the local laughingstock."

"No, you won't." Gabe moved to the side of her chair and crouched next to it as one hand covered hers. "They genuinely care about you."

"Uh-huh." She closed her eyes and wished she were anywhere but here.

"They do." His hand moved to her chin and tilted it. "Look at me, Blair."

"Yes?" She glared at him angrily.

"Did you ever think that some of those people could do a better job than you? That they were just waiting to be asked to help, to be needed? That they wanted to feel a part of things but were afraid to volunteer for fear they wouldn't measure up to your standard?"

She frowned. "No, I can honestly say I never thought that," she muttered, anger nipping at her tangled emotions. "You make me sound like Attila the Hun."

He shook his head, his eyes dancing as he inspected her body when she lay back on the chair. "I don't think so." He laughed. "More like Mary Poppins. Capable of anything." He stood and pulled her up beside him, hugging her close for just a moment. "I know you can do it all, and you know you can do it all, but let's not tell everyone, okay? It makes them nervous.''

After a moment Blair pulled away, chin thrust out as she glared at him. "You're not off the hook that easily,'' she muttered. "What you're saying is that I tend to take over.''

He nodded soberly. "Like a bulldozer. Not that you don't have to sometimes. But not right now.''

"And not when there are people, capable people who could do it far better.'' She sneaked a glance upward and caught an odd look on his face. "Just how did you know about all these things, anyway?'' she demanded.

Gabe's arm fell away from her waist. He reached up and took a sheet of silver-gray paper from his shirt pocket—paper that she'd left on her dressing table this morning.

"Ronnie Morris is doing the canvassing. Tina George will take the kids to camp. Maddie and Stu are taking your place as Sunday morning greeters at church. Somebody named Elfie has taken over the Sunday school picnic, and Tatiana—'' he glanced up, a frown twitching at the corner of his mouth "—is that right?''

Blair stuffed down the giggle and nodded.

Gabe continued reading from his note. "Tatiana has been conscripted to help out with the Kids' Crusade.'' He folded the note carefully and handed it to her. "Are you angry?''

"Should I be?'' She kept her face solemn, her eyes serious. "You walk in, take over my life and reorganize it all in one half hour. How would you feel?''

"Mad,'' he confirmed, shoulders slumping as he walked to his chair and sank into it disconsolately.

"I'd say I'm sorry, but I'm not. You were doing too much." His face hardened. "And you know it."

Blair walked to the edge of the pool and sat near his chair. She dangled her legs in the water. "Yes, I do know it," she admitted finally.

"Huh?" He got up from his chair, walked around it and sank down beside her. "Did I hear that correctly?"

"Don't push it," she warned, but there was a smile in her voice.

He wrapped his arm around her shoulders and hugged her. "Thank you for not raking me over the coals," he whispered against her ear. "I just wanted some time for us to bond as a family, and I couldn't see how we were going to do it if you were never here."

"I was here." She looked up and caught the pained look on his face. "All right! I was gone a lot. I thought I was helping them."

"You *were* helping them." He hugged her again, and his mouth brushed against her forehead. There was a lightness in his voice, a tenderness in his touch that told her he wanted to do more. "But we need help, too."

She sighed. "I know I'm possessive about my business," she murmured, allowing herself to relax against him for a moment. "I guess I'm such a control freak because I'm so scared of messing up."

Gabe pulled away, holding her at arm's length as he stared at her. "Messing up? You?" He shook his head in mock reproof, but his voice was confident, brimming with assurance. "You're not going to fail at anything, sweetheart. You can do or be whatever you need, if not with the candles and honey, then with something else. You don't have to prove to me that you're a success. I already believe it.'' He drew her close once more. ''I just wish that you did.''

Blair closed her eyes and relished being held so tenderly. It had been so long, so very long since she'd felt protected, cared for, *cherished*. She reflected on the word for a moment. Yes, that was it. Cherished. When Gabe held her like this she felt delicate, but oh, so strong. She felt protected, yet ready to defend. She felt—loved.

''What do you mean—you wish I believed it?'' She barely whispered the words, hating to break the spell.

''I think you're trying to prove yourself, Blair. Isn't that what all this frenetic activity is about—showing everyone that you can do it, that you can handle whatever you get? Mother, granddaughter, niece, friend, church member, businesswoman.'' He stopped a moment. ''Superwoman,'' he said, holding her away so he could look into her eyes. ''Isn't that it?''

She shrugged, pulling away. He was getting a little too close for comfort.

''I think it is. But don't you see, honey? It doesn't matter to Mac or Willie or Albert, but especially to Daniel, that you've got all these irons in the fire. First and foremost, what Daniel wants is his mommy there when he wants her.''

She listened to him without speaking.

''You were wrong, you know.'' Gabe pressed her head against his chest and swept his hand down the length of her damp hair. ''There is no such thing as making quality time. You can't make it. It happens in those moments when you're relaxed and not really thinking about anything. That's when the enlightenment comes, the questions are asked, the biggest de-

cisions are made. You can't schedule that. I should
know.''

"Why?'' she whispered, so afraid to break this sa-
cred time but needing to pull away, to regain her equi-
librium. She drew back, but left her arms wrapped
around his waist.

"For the first few weeks after my mother died, my
father used to make me sit down for a half hour every
day after dinner, if he was home. I had to tell him
everything I'd done that day. If I missed something,
I'd hear about it later.'' He sighed, fiddling with her
curls, wrapping them around his finger and then
watching as they sprang away.

"I suppose he thought he was making time for me.
What it really felt like was an interrogation. I never
did tell him how scared I was of the school bully, or
that I hated art class.''

He laughed, but to Blair, there was no humor in it.

"I wanted so badly to tell him that Mom usually
let me pick out one shirt, a special one. And that I
wanted a red shirt, a bright red one. Stupid little
things that we might have discussed while we were
playing at something or sitting together.''

She tilted her head to meet his eyes. "That's what
you want with Daniel, isn't it? That time of quiet
confidences?''

"I want him to feel that he can trust me with anything. That's the way I want you to feel, too. But we
need time together to build that trust.''

She sighed, acknowledging the truth of what he'd
said. "I know.''

"You don't have to prove anything to me, Blair.''
His hands held her head so she couldn't look away
from that steady regard. "I don't care much what

other people think. I *know,* or at least I'm beginning
to know who you are deep inside.'' His voice dropped
to a gruff whisper as he set her away and stepped into
the pool.

''You don't have to half kill yourself to prove to
me that you could get along just fine without my help,
Blair. Believe me, I already know that. You've
proven it for seven years.''

As she watched him submerge himself into the water, eyes squeezed tightly closed, Blair felt her throat
tighten up. He thought she only tolerated his presence,
that she didn't need him to be in Daniel's life, to be
in *her* life.

How had she ever made him believe such a terrible
lie?

Chapter Ten

Blair shifted on the tiled edge of the pool, prepared to go to Gabe, to swallow her pride and tell him how wrong he was, to admit she needed him now more than she ever had.

"Mommy! Daddy! Guess what?"

Daniel's excited voice checked the impulse, and Blair stayed put. She would deal with this later, she decided. During some of that time Gabe wanted them to spend together.

"We're out here, son. By the pool."

Gabe emerged from yet another dousing and paddled his way from the deeper water to the shallow.

"Daniel's home," she told him.

In the second that he absorbed her words, Gabriel Sloan transformed right before her eyes. His eyes lit up, and his mouth lost the tense, tight line that held it captive. He climbed the steps eagerly, snatching a towel to dry as Daniel hurled himself through the door that led off the kitchen.

"Are you guys swimming *now?*" he asked, big

eyes round with amazement. "Don't you have to work, Mom?"

Blair cringed inwardly, then forced out a laugh. "Not right now. Right now we're taking a rest." She held out her arms and pulled him close when he ran into them. "Boy, you've grown again. I can feel it." She pushed the hair off his face and smiled. "What's got you grinning?"

"Teacher said to ask if we could look after Babycakes until next fall. She'll take him back when she returns from her summer trip. Can we, Mom? I'd take good care of him. I promise." Daniel crossed his heart, his eyes pleading with her just as his father's had mere moments before.

Blair considered it. "I don't know," she murmured. She tilted her head to stare at Gabe. "Maybe we'd better ask your dad what he thinks."

Daniel raced over to the big man and flung himself into arms he seemed to know would be waiting for him. "Can I, Daddy?"

Gabe snuggled him on his lap in a nearby chair, then frowned. "I don't know," he said.

"I promise I'll take really good care of him. You won't even know he's here. I'll feed him and water him, and take him for walks lots so he doesn't get into any trouble. He can't stay at his own house anymore 'cause they're moving away. And their new place don't allow no dogs. Can I?"

It whooshed out in a jumbled mass of begging and promises that made Blair grin. Especially when she caught sight of Gabe's face.

"What or who is a Babycakes?" he asked, one eyebrow tilted.

"A dog, silly." Daniel grinned at his father as if he were teasing. "You know that. I tole you before."

"Oh. Yes. Babycakes, the dog. Right." Gabe blinked, then turned to Blair with a shrug that screamed, "Help!"

"A very large dog. An English sheepdog. A blind English sheepdog." Blair kept her lips pinched together. This organized, helpful man was in for a surprise if he thought Babycakes was a regular dog. "He's sort of the kids' mascot. They all love him. Some folks in town found him early this spring and have let him stay on their farm. But they're moving."

"Oh." Clearly Gabe didn't know whether to say yes or no. His eyes begged her to help out.

"Can we have him here for the summer, Mommy? Ple-e-e-ease." Daniel dragged the plea out to a twelve letter word.

"Babycakes is a boy dog." Blair hid her grin behind her hand. "I don't know, Daniel. I guess it will be up to your father to decide that. I promised him I wouldn't take on any other jobs. He thinks you miss me too much."

Temporarily diverted, Daniel nodded. "I did miss you last night, Mommy. You always come and kiss me good-night."

"I did last night, too," she whispered, her eyes filling with tears. "It's just that you didn't see me because your eyes were closed. All scrunched up. Like this." She made a face and honked a loud snore.

"I was sleeping!" Daniel giggled, wiggling to get a look at his dad. "Wasn't I?"

"If that obnoxious noise can be called sleeping." Gabe tickled Daniel, then glanced over his head at Blair. "Is this dog thing okay with you?"

She got up, sauntered up the stairs, then paused at the door to the bedroom. She forced her face into a mask of seriousness and turned to face him.

"I'm leaving that up to you." When his eyes widened at her simpering tone, she smiled. "I don't want to volunteer for anything more. My husband might think he was being ignored. I wouldn't want the town gossiping about that. Would you?" She stepped regally into the room and swept the French doors closed behind her, snicking the lock into place.

"Oh, boy, are you in for a surprise, Gabe." She stepped under the shower, her mind busy with a picture of Babycakes loose in the castle. "A really big surprise. If you thought we were busy before, you ain't seen nothing yet."

In the process, Gabe might just discover how very much she needed him right by her side.

He wanted her to trust him? Then that's exactly what she'd do. Blair sincerely hoped her husband knew what he was asking for.

"Would somebody please get this stupid animal off of me?"

Friday morning, Gabe's muffled protests carried through the open kitchen window where Blair was mixing a batch of cookies.

"Please?"

She stifled the burble of laughter that itched to be set free and walked to the patio doors. Gabe lay on the grass, his body swathed by the big woolly body of a wriggling, ecstatically happy dog who busied himself licking his face and anything else within range of his lolling pink tongue. Babycakes. Again.

With a grimace of remorse for the forget-me-nots

they'd ruined, Blair shoved open the screen and stepped out.

"What are you doing, Gabe?" she inquired mildly.

"I *was* walking. Minding my own business. He got me from behind and knocked me over. Do you mind? I've been lying here begging for help for at least ten minutes." He quickly averted his face as the pink tongue swept across it once more. "Blair, please!"

"I love it when you beg." She put two fingers in her mouth, curled her tongue and whistled for all she was worth.

Babycakes rolled onto his back, legs poking straight up in the air as he froze in position. Gabe scrambled to his feet, rescued his sunglasses from underneath his rear quarters, his cell phone from under his left ear, then marched across the grass to where Blair stood.

"I'm a mess."

"You certainly are." She moved to snap the leash on the dog and led him to the fenced-in area Gabe had constructed two days ago. The dog sat obediently while she unsnapped the leash, then trotted to his water dish. Blair closed the heavy gate with a sigh.

"He hasn't been here a week and we've lost just about every flower. If Mac catches him tiptoeing through the petunias, he'll be sorry." She fixed Gabe with a glare. "So will you. Why did you let him out?"

"I didn't!" His indignant glare convinced her. "That *thing* was lying on the deck sunning. I thought I could sneak past him and I almost made it." He grimaced at the hair covering his elegant black suit pants.

"Why are you all dressed up?" Blair asked, latching the screen.

"I told you, remember? I have to make a quick trip to L.A. Something's happening and they want me back for a couple of hours. I should be home by seven." He made a face at the slobber that covered his sunglasses. "That animal is a menace."

"You told Daniel he could have him here," she reminded him pertly, enjoying this side of the perfectly groomed, always impeccable Gabriel Sloan. "Can't very well change your mind now." She concentrated on forming the little balls of peanut butter dough. "This is the second time this week you've had to go. Is there a problem?"

Gabe shook his head, though his eyes didn't meet hers. "No, just a glitch. Shouldn't take long."

"Now where have I heard that before?" Blair switched the pans in the oven, setting the pan loaded with golden brown discs to cool on the counter. "Last time went considerably longer than you expected. Good thing you picked today. Daniel's still at that sleepover. He'll stay until supper time. By then he should be extra tired."

"Have you got everything you need for his party tomorrow? Anything I can pick up?" He reached out, snagged one of the cookies, blew on it, then popped it into his mouth. "Mmm." He huffed and puffed for a minute, letting the heat dissipate as he chewed, swallowed, then grinned at her. "Very good."

"You're supposed to eat them in bites," Blair scolded, pushing the pan away so he couldn't reach any more. "You know, actually *taste* them?"

Gabe flicked her ponytail, slipped an arm around her shoulders and tugged her close for a quick kiss.

"I did taste them. They taste great," he murmured, his face inches from hers. "So do you."

"Oh, my! I didn't realize I'd be interrupting." Willie stood in the doorway, eyes sparkling. She made no attempt to leave, but stood inspecting Blair's hurried exit from her husband's embrace. "Don't bother on my account. I expected a lot more canoodling from a pair of newlyweds than I've seen from you two."

Blair wanted to groan. She ached to scream a denial, drop her apron on the counter and tear off across the valley to a quiet spot where her emotions didn't do these strange acrobatics, a place where her brain functioned normally instead of sending out little snaps of electricity whenever Gabe came near.

Neither screaming nor leaving was an option with Daniel's cake left to bake. So Blair focused on the job at hand and slid the cookies from the baking sheet to a rack.

"Gabriel, you have white stuff on the seat of those elegant pants." Willie giggled. "Are you going somewhere?" Her voice laughed across the room in a tumbling cadence of genuine pleasure that Blair hadn't heard enough of lately.

"Yes, Willie, I am. I have to make a quick trip to L.A. There's a small problem with my company there, and I need to attend a meeting." He craned his neck and plucked another dog hair off his pants, his mouth stretching in a grimace of displeasure. "If I can get out of here without being attacked again, that is."

"I'm sure Blair didn't mean to attack you," Willie murmured, her back turned as she studied Daniel's elaborate picture of a train cake on licorice tracks. She'd promised to ice the confection if Blair would bake it. "Say you're sorry, dear."

Blair made a face at Gabe. "I'm sorry." She parroted the words without the least bit of sincerity.

"Yes, I can see that." Gabe smirked at her raised eyebrows. "Can I get anything for the party?" he repeated. "I mean, maybe the car isn't enough. It's not..."

Blair set her hands on her hips and glared at him. "A *car* isn't enough for a six-year-old? Enough of this, Gabriel. You can't buy Daniel. As it is you're spoiling him silly. What other six-year-old kid has a toy car to drive around a castle? Hmm?"

She considered the bright red bicycle hidden in Albert's workshop. She'd scrimped and saved to buy it. It had taken months of careful, frugal planning. Without even considering *her* wishes, Gabe had eclipsed that gift a hundred times over.

"I wasn't trying to buy him." The happy banter drained away from Gabe's low voice.

"Well, that's what it looks like from here." Blair stubbornly turned her back on him and rolled out more cookies. Frustration clamored for release as she considered the day to come.

Daniel's sixth birthday. A day she'd planned for ages, long before Gabe had come on the scene. She'd planned to take the kids on a hike up near Lake Timco. They would have a campfire, a wiener roast, sing silly songs, go on a treasure hunt. But Gabriel's arrival had changed all that.

Now Daniel wanted a pool party. The hike and wiener roast had been done before. Steven B.'s party last month was a treasure hunt and *everybody* had wieners. But nobody else had a pool.

Blair sighed. Would Daniel even *want* to ride a bicycle when he could drive a car?

The silence in the room drew her from her reflections. Willie turned from her cake study. A sad look filled her eyes as she studied Blair's rigid backbone. "Excuse me," she whispered after a moment. "My head hurts."

Once she'd left, the tension grew enormously. Blair knew it was her fault. Gabe was doing his best, trying exceptionally hard to be the father he wanted to be. But she couldn't accept that, couldn't just allow him to walk in and take over their lives. Not completely.

She forced herself to keep on working.

"I'm not trying to overshadow you, Blair. Or show off." Defeat edged the solemn words. "I guess we should have talked it over before I ordered the car. I didn't realize you'd have objections, but now that I look at this from your perspective, I'm beginning to understand."

He walked to her, gently turned her so she had to look at him.

"You probably had all kinds of plans for his birthday long before I showed up." He winced, catching sight of the truth she knew was reflected in her woe-begone face. "And his gift, too?"

Blair wanted desperately to pretend that it didn't matter. She wanted to be blasé, to pretend an airy nonchalance so he wouldn't see how much it stung. She wanted him to believe it didn't matter that he was usurping her.

But it did matter. It mattered a lot.

She nodded.

He closed his eyes and tilted his head so his chin touched her forehead. "I'm sorry," he muttered, his fingers on her shoulders drawing her closer. "I should have checked with you before I barged full steam ahead.''

"It's all right." It cost her dearly to say that. Blair kept her eyes closed so he wouldn't see how much.

"No, it isn't."

She blinked her eyes open and stared as Gabe stepped back, his arms falling to his sides. He shook his head.

"No, it isn't. I keep doing this! Why don't I learn?"

She felt silly and childish as she watched the worry crowd out the joy that had filled his face short moments ago. "You probably put a lot of thought into that car."

"Yes, I did." His troubled eyes studied her. "I wanted to make a big splash, to give him something to remember. The first year his father was there for his birthday." One lip curled. "Go ahead, call me selfish."

"I wasn't going to say that." *Liar.*

"Weren't you?" He raked a hand through his perfectly cropped dark hair. "Then you're more charitable than I. I'll take the car back."

"No!" Blair gaped. He couldn't mean it. Give up the gift every little boy dreamed of? Because of her?

"Yes. We should have decided on something together. Knowing you, you'd have weighed all the pros and cons until you came up with a perfectly planned gift." He shrugged into his jacket. "What did you pick out?"

"A bike." She couldn't believe what she'd done. How had it happened? One moment she was mad because Gabe was trying to usurp her position as

Daniel's mother, the next thing she knew, she'd made her son's father rescind his gift.

"That's probably exactly what he needs." Gabe nodded as he considered it. "Yes, it's perfect. That way he can ride down to the neighbors to play for an hour. A boy should have a bike. It can go anywhere. The car would have only worked on the driveway." Gabe tugged out his wallet. "Can I pay for half? That way it would be from both of us."

"Of course, if you want. But what about..." Blair didn't know what to say. She watched as Gabe laid two crisp one-hundred-dollar bills on the counter. "It didn't cost that much."

"Whatever." He shrugged, stuffing his wallet into his pocket and managing to check his watch as he did. "I've got to go. The jet's waiting at the airport. I'll call the delivery people to pick up the car. It was a silly idea, anyway."

"It wasn't silly." *I was.* She felt small, nitpicky. She'd ruined something special, a happy memory. She'd stolen it from him as surely as she'd accused him of trying to do the same to her. Unlike her, Gabe seemed to hold no grudges.

He snatched his briefcase, gave her a quick kiss on the cheek and strode toward the door. "Whatever happens, I'll be back tonight," he told her. "I won't miss tomorrow. Not for anything."

Blair moved to the window and watched him leave.

Selfish, her conscience chastised. *Have to have everything your own way. Try to shut him out if you will, but Daniel still needs a father. You're only hurting him, your own son.*

She squeezed her eyes shut, forced the tears back and turned to the cookies.

"I can't lose him," she whispered. "I can't let Gabe buy his love."

"Are you sure that's what he was doing?" Mac leaned against the door frame, his face reproving. "Are you certain Gabe wasn't giving Daniel something he wanted, fulfilling a fantasy of his own?"

"I suppose Willie told you." Blair tugged out the mixing bowl and began assembling the ingredients for Daniel's cake.

"He's lonely, Blair. He's been lonely for a very long time."

"Gabriel Sloan has always had hordes of people at his beck and call." She cracked the eggs so hard, bits of eggshell slid into the bowl. She fished desperately for the elusive pieces.

"Not someone special," Mac reminded her. "Not someone who cared for him. Not someone of his own."

Blair dumped the eggs down the drain and started again. The words stung. *Someone of his own.*

"Daniel isn't just your son. He's Gabe's child as much as he is yours. You can't deny that, and you can't make it go away. You've got to accept reality, Blair. You've got to learn to trust him. Gabe isn't going away."

She dumped in a cup of sugar and started the mixer. "He just did," she muttered, certain her grandfather wouldn't hear.

Mac heard. "Not for good." His voice was raised sharply against the noise. Mac frowned. "He'll be back, Busy Bee. He'll always be back. This is his home now."

"Is it?" Blair studied the certainty on her grandfather's face for a moment. "How do you know that?'' she demanded, turning away to add vanilla and melted chocolate.

When Mac didn't answer, she stopped what she was doing and turned off the machine. Her grandfather stood by the patio doors, peering over the smooth, clear surface of the pool.

Perhaps he hadn't heard her. "How do you know, Grandpa?''

Mac turned to face her, his mouth stretched in a beatific grin of smug satisfaction.

"Because he said so. And Gabe always keeps his promises.''

Would he?

She grabbed the flour canister and measured two and one half cups. She stirred cocoa into the wet mixture. She heated water to dissolve the baking soda. But still the thoughts pricked at her.

On our wedding day, he promised to love me. Can Gabe keep that promise?

Chapter Eleven

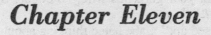

Gabe leaned back in his upholstered first-class seat and closed his eyes. Ten o'clock. L.A. was just coming alive and he was dead tired. No wonder, he was on mountain time. As soon as the plane gained cruising altitude and leveled off, he pulled out his cell phone and dialed. He needed a reality check.

"Hi, Jake. It's me. Leaving L.A. Another meeting."

"So how were the meetings?"

"Boring. Deadly dull and boring. Who cares if we gained two more points on the index or if some Korean firm is looking at a major purchase."

Jake chuckled. "I take it there was someplace else you'd rather have been?"

Gabe closed his eyes and thought of Daniel racing in the door from his friend's house. The three of them could have gone for a walk, watched the sun go down, even swam together. Lately Blair had taken to sitting outside in the hot tub long after everyone else had gone to bed. He watched her there, night after night, wondering if she'd welcome his presence. Maybe tonight she'd have told him to stay, to talk for a while. He ached for those words.

"Is this a bad connection or are you daydreaming?"

Gabe winced at Jake's snappy retort. "Daydreaming," he confessed.

"About your gorgeous wife, no doubt? So how is paradise?"

"Messed up." Gabe hated thinking about how stupid he'd been. He'd almost drooled imagining Daniel's expression when he saw that car sitting on the drive with his name on it. Gabe hadn't spared one thought for the way Blair must have felt, the weeks of pinching pennies he knew she must have done so she could get that bike.

"Okay, what did you do this time?" Jake's tone brimmed with long-suffering patience.

Gabe told him the whole story. "I always think about myself first, Jake, about how I'll look. It's the same reason I had to live in L.A. I thought people would take me more seriously if I had just the right address, came from the ritzy part of town, knew the right people." He felt the weight of his stupidity. "I didn't stop to reason out why, or to imagine how it might come across to Blair. I just wanted to show my son that I could get him whatever he wanted."

"And did Daniel want *that* car?"

Gabe swallowed, shifted the phone to his other ear and admitted the truth. "I don't think he even knew it existed until I showed him a picture in a catalogue. After I explained how fast it could go and all the rest, he got excited." Gabe nodded at the copilot and accepted a cup of coffee.

Jake didn't say anything for a long time. Then his quiet voice probed a little deeper. "What's really bothering you, Gabe?"

The window by his elbow gave a view of inky blackness. Gabe could discern nothing, no city lights, no ground cover, nothing. Clouds obliterated the view. It was exactly like his life. No matter how hard he tried, the future he imagined just wouldn't materialize.

"Daniel's a replica of his mother. He isn't impressed much by things," he admitted finally. "He doesn't seem affected by expensive toys or new clothes. Even by the castle. He likes the pool, but I get the feeling the river would work just as well. All he seems to care about is whether or not Blair and I are there."

Jake shouted with laughter. "That's the way it's supposed to be, bud."

"Yeah, I know." Gabe swallowed a mouthful of coffee that he didn't want, brooding on the whole puzzle. "But it's exactly the opposite of who I am. Today Blair accused me of trying to buy Daniel's love with the car."

"Was she right?" Trust Jake to hit where it hurt.

"I don't know. But the more I think about it, the more I'm afraid she was." Gabe thought about her last night, curled up on the cold, dirty ground beside Daniel, trying to coax a squirrel to take some bread from her hand. "I made sure I took care of her family, got her a decent place to live. I bugged her about working so hard, trying to make her see she's killing herself with worry. I thought I was doing all the right things that men are supposed to do when they want to build a family."

"And?"

"None of it matters." Suddenly Gabe didn't want to pretend anymore. "Willie goes to the old house almost every day. I followed her once. She sits on the porch and stares into space. Then, when she gets too hot or thirsty, she comes back. I didn't tell Blair, but I think her illness is getting worse. She seems to space right out." He took a deep breath. "Mac goes there when he thinks Willie and Blair aren't looking. He pretends it's to help Albert, but it isn't. He sits on a bale of hay by the barn and chews on a piece of straw. In between he whistles."

"Whistles?" Even Jake seemed surprised.

"Uh-huh. That song, 'Beautiful Dreamer,' he whistles it for ages. Over and over and over. He walks to the top of the hill, stares out over the valley for a long time, then goes home. It's weird."

"Why?"

"Because they keep leaving the new home they're in for the old ramshackle one they've left." Gabe shifted as the hurt burned deep inside. What more could he do? Was he losing the only family he'd ever had?

"Perhaps they have some fond memories of the old place. Perhaps they feel more comfortable there."

"But why?" Gabe pushed the cup away. He didn't need more coffee. He needed answers. "I've given them everything they could ask for. Blair will never want for a thing."

"Except maybe love. You've made them beholden, Jake. You haven't loved them."

Gabe closed his eyes as the truth of the words slammed home. "I can't change that, Jake," he whispered. "I'm not that kind of man."

"Aren't you? Then you need to pray for God to change you. Because the Bible says we're to love our neighbor as ourselves. And that comes right after we love God with all our hearts, all our minds, all our souls, all our strength." He waited a moment, then grumbled his disgust. "Did you hear me, Gabe?"

"Yeah, I heard."

"Then you know the Bible doesn't say we should *try* to love. It doesn't say we should squeeze our eyes closed, take a deep breath and hope we can do it. It says love. It's a command. And if God said it, you can do it."

The fear rose inside him like a mountain of gall, choking him until he could barely say the word. "How?"

"Let go of yourself. Stop thinking about how great you are to do this, how much you can do, how much you've provided, how they should appreciate you. Take you out of the picture. Loving is about the other person. What they want, what they need, what they feel."

"I don't think I can do that, Jake," Gabe said sadly.

Jake laughed. "You've already started. You were concerned at the thought that you were trying to buy Daniel's affection. That's love, Gabe. Call it what you want. You don't want Willie or Mac to suffer alone on the old home place. That's caring, Gabriel." He chuckled, the sound twinkling over the airwaves straight to Gabe's heart. "You want Blair to approve of you, to commend you, to appreciate you. In my book, that's love."

"But—"

"'And He who has begun a good work in you will

not stop until it is complete.' That's the Bible, buddy. God's word on the subject. He's working on teaching you love, and He's not going to stop until you learn the whole lesson.''

Gabe felt the slight shift in air pressure and knew they were nearing their destination. ''Don't you ever get tired of being right?'' he complained.

''Nope.'' Jake laughed at his snarl of disgust. ''What you have to do, Gabriel, is put the people first. Forget about everything else. After the people, the rest just doesn't matter. You've married into a family who is smart about these things. They already know what to value. People come first. In thirty years, is Daniel going to remember what he got for his sixth birthday, or is he going to remember that his parents were there, laughing and celebrating with him?''

Prompted by the captain's flashing light, Gabe quickly thanked his friend and said goodbye.

As they descended, then taxied into the airport, he made himself replay Jake's words.

Think about them.

So if he was Blair, in a strange house, married to someone who'd always put his money first, what would he do now?

The answer hit him hard.

Blair was the kind of woman who'd wait and see if the other person was trustworthy. She'd bide her time until she was certain she wouldn't be betrayed again.

It was ironic. If it were him in her position, Gabe knew he'd be long gone. In his books, nobody got a second chance.

You did.

The reminder that God had given him much more

than one second chance burned like indigestion. Didn't it behoove him to cut everybody else a little slack? Wasn't it time to stop expecting everyone to applaud him, and start finding out who his family really was?

Gabe let himself into the silent darkened house and set his briefcase near the door.

He moved through the house. The train cake sat proud and colorful in the center of the dining room table, its cars following behind in black- and red-iced abandon. Peanut butter cookies spilled out of the cookie jar and onto a huge tray on the counter.

Gabe tucked three into a napkin, poured himself a glass of milk and headed onto the patio to think over Jake's words. He grinned. It felt good to be back, to be home.

A shadowed figure in the hot tub slowed his steps. "Blair?"

She turned to face him, her features barely discernible in the dim light. "Hi."

"Hi, yourself. How long have you been sitting here?"

She shrugged, waiting until he pulled his chair nearer. "I don't know. A while. I guess I got lost in my thoughts. Couldn't sleep."

"What kind of thoughts?" He couldn't stop the shiver of apprehension that twitched in his brain.

"Actually, I was thinking about what you said the other day." Her head came up, her eyes steady as they met his, dark and glowing in the light from the bottom of the tub. "You said you knew that Daniel and I didn't need you. That's not entirely true."

He took a bite of cookie, more for something to do

than because he was hungry. All his nerves stood at attention as he waited for her to continue. *Please, God, don't let her tell me to go. Not now. Not yet!*

"I can imagine how difficult it must have been for you to handle everything, Blair. It's pretty clear that you were doing just fine on your own." He swallowed. "I'm well aware that my presence causes you stress, like impulsively buying that car. That was stupid."

He risked a glance at her and saw she was studying him, a faint smile tugging the corners of her mouth.

"That was brilliant," she muttered. "And if I hadn't been so selfish and petty, I'd have told you that right off. Daniel will love it."

"But, I thought—"

"I couldn't send it back! It's *your* gift to him. Who am I to set up conditions and terms about what you should give your own son? I've always wanted the best for Daniel and now that he's getting it, I'm afraid I have a bad case of sour grapes." She shifted so that the jets pummeled her back. "I'm sorry I did that, Gabe. It was rude."

He stared at her, unable to believe what she was saying. "I shouldn't have presumed to pick out his gift," he mumbled.

"Why not?" Her head tilted, topknot wobbling dangerously as she frowned. "Most fathers pick out a gift for their sons. Why should you be any different?" She laughed, a harsh sound that gave him a clue to the bitterness she felt. "I'm still under construction, Gabe, and God is having a tough time teaching me humility."

"Why should you be humble?" He leaned forward,

elbows on his knees. "You haven't done anything to be ashamed of."

"Haven't I?" She gave an odd little laugh that seemed to jerk out of her. "Do you know why I was so mad?"

He shrugged. "I didn't consult you. I ruined your plans. I took over. Take your pick."

Slowly she shook her head. Gabe was fascinated by the movement, fully appreciative of the lovely picture she made, neck rising from the steaming water like a regal swan's. "Believe me, Blair, I know my faults."

"I was mad because you showed me up." Her words hit the night air with a hard, bitter sound. "You went out and bought this shiny car that I knew Daniel would fawn over and all I had was that measly bike to offer."

He gulped, totally fazed by her blunt admittance. "Consciously, I really wasn't trying to buy his love, Blair, though I guess if we look at base motives, that was in there."

Her hands smacked the water, sending a spray of droplets in a wide arc that managed to hit his pants and spatter his shirt.

"Stop being so self-effacing, will you?" Her voice brimmed with frustration. "I'm trying to apologize."

"Oh." He waited until he thought it was safe, then nodded. "Okay then, I'll accept yours if you'll accept mine. You're the best mother my son could ever have. I wouldn't do anything to jeopardize his happiness." He made sure she was looking at him. "I never meant to show you up, Blair."

"Do you think I don't know that? Well, at least I

figured it out once I got over my anger.'' She shifted to a higher step.

Gabe watched as the steam rose off her shoulders in a thick white mist, but he held his tongue. She was telling him something. He needed to listen.

''In case you haven't noticed, I'm not very secure in my position as Daniel's mother, not with you around.'' She didn't look at him.

''Can you tell me why?''

Blair sighed. ''It's stupid! I feel as if I've been scrounging just to make ends meet and then in you walk and in one fell swoop, manage to make his dreams come true. All I managed was to put food on the table.'' She glanced sideways at him, then away.

It wasn't much, but Gabe caught the flash of hurt in her eyes and called himself a fool. He'd stepped all over her pride with his high-handed methods, his determination to make up for the past. He owed her for that.

''Blair?'' When she kept her eyes on the wooden bridge over the creek, stubbornly refusing to look at him, Gabe knew what he had to do. He slipped off his shoes and socks, then stepped into the tub to sit beside her, his arm sliding around her shoulders. ''Listen to me, Blair.''

She stared at him in disbelief, glancing from his sodden clothes to his face with bewilderment clouding her gorgeous eyes. ''What are you doing, Gabe? You'll ruin those clothes!''

''This is more important.'' He grasped her chin in his hand and stared into her eyes. ''You gave Daniel everything, Blair. You gave him life, then you loved him enough for both of us. You protected him, you cared for him, you made sure he had everything a little boy could need. Nothing I could buy would ever compare to that, and I know it. So does Daniel.''

Shiny silver tears gathered on the tips of her thick brown lashes as she stared at him. Her liquid chocolate eyes filled and overflowed, sending the tears tumbling down her cheeks.

''Thank you,'' she whispered in a broken sob. Then she threw herself into his arms, her own going around him in a viselike grip that punched Gabe in the stomach.

He brushed a hand over her hair, tugging the comb free so that the glossy strands tumbled down in a riot of bouncy curls. His lips found the velvet cord in her neck and he brushed it tenderly.

''I don't know how you can stand me,'' she whimpered against his throat. ''I've been so mean, so arrogant. All this time I've been trying to make you pay for something that was never your fault.''

The truth crystallized in his mind. ''It was my fault, Blair. I should never have allowed things to get out of control. I knew it was wrong, but I let passion overrule my conscience.'' He nuzzled a little closer. ''But I've prayed for forgiveness and I believe God's given it. Now I need to ask for yours.'' He moved her away until he could stare into her eyes.

''Will you forgive me for that night, Blair? And for all the mistakes I've made since?''

She nodded slowly, her words, when they came, whisper soft. ''I have to.''

He moved her hair so he could see every angle and curve of her beautiful face. ''No, you don't have to,'' he corrected her. ''You could go on hating me forever, and I'd deserve it.''

As he watched, a light from within began to glow

in the depths of her eyes. They stayed focused steadily on him while her head turned from left to right.

"I don't hate you, Gabriel Sloan."

He whooshed out a sigh of relief and closed his eyes. He leaned until his forehead pressed against hers, searching for some way to tell her what her forgiveness meant.

"I can't hate you. I love you, Gabe. I always have."

His head jerked up as he searched those shiny depths, desperately craving the truth.

"I love you more than life. It just took me a while to realize it." She smiled, one hand lifting to touch his cheek, to brush against the stubble on his chin, smooth the furrow of confusion across his forehead. "I always thought my love for you was a mistake, a childish infatuation. Something I'd grown out of. I was wrong."

"Wh-what are you saying?" He could barely breathe.

"Is it so hard to accept?" she murmured, her innocent eyes laughing into his. "I love you. That's why I wanted to marry you then. That's why I married you now. I tried to hide it, tried to pretend it wasn't real. But I realized today that my pretending only builds walls between us." She leaned forward and kissed him tenderly, her lips featherlight against his. "I want Daniel to know you, to love you the way a child loves and adores his father. I want him to depend on you, to trust you, to run to you when he needs help."

"I'm not a very good father, Blair." It was the only thing that he could say. Fear clutched his throat.

"You're a wonderful father, Gabe. You care about Daniel, you want the best for him. You won't let him down, you'll always do your best to see that he gets what he needs. You're fair and understanding and patient. You love him."

The words pierced his heart like a white-hot arrow, tunneling to the very core of him. Was it true? Was it love, this fierce need to make sure Daniel never wanted for anything, never felt alone or abandoned? Had love made him walk out of that meeting before it was over so he could be here for his son's sixth birthday?

"I know because that's exactly the way I feel about him, too." She smiled at the confusion Gabe knew was written all over his face.

"But that doesn't mean..." He stopped, unwilling to say it aloud, just in case it was true and he'd spoil it all.

"That doesn't mean I love you?" She laughed softly. "I loved you long ago, Gabe. When you were dragging me to all those Hollywood parties, I knew. I only went because I could see that it meant a lot to you, and I didn't want to spoil it for you."

"But how can you forgive me for letting you walk away? For asking you to do something you felt was wrong?" He didn't understand this, didn't want to trust in it, to believe that such forgiveness existed.

"How can I not?" She linked her fingers in his, her forefinger pressing against the wedding band she'd slipped on his hand mere weeks ago. "'By this will all men know that you are My disciples, if you have love one for another.' How can I not love you when God loves and forgives me?"

"It sounds too easy." He frowned, waiting for that steady glow to die in her eyes.

"I know. That's exactly what I said to God. It's too easy. He should pay for forcing me to leave, to have Daniel alone. It's not fair."

Gabe waited, knowing she wasn't finished. His fingers couldn't help but touch her hair, burying themselves in its glossy fullness. To be near Blair was to touch her.

"I sat here, full of anger and bitterness, pouting. Then the truth hit me. God's son died for me. Was that fair?" She smiled, the tears coursing down her cheeks as she shook her head.

"I'm sorry, Gabe. From here on in, I'm letting go of the grudges, the complaints, the bitterness. It's forgiven. I don't care what you've done or what happened in the past." Her mouth split wide in a smile of pure joy. "I love you."

Gabe couldn't stop himself from basking in that light any more than he could prevent his arms from wrapping themselves around her and pulling her so close he thought he'd never let go.

As her arms fit around his neck and drew his head to hers, a deep sense of peace washed over him. He'd waited for this for so long, wanted to be held like this so many times. How often had he watched her and yearned to hold her in his arms, to immerse himself in a love like this. To feel as if he belonged.

The doubts crept in, clawing their way into the circle that held them together.

"What if I mess up?" he whispered, his hands tight around her. "What if I can't be the husband or father you want?"

Blair's long, elegant fingers slid from his shoulders

to cup his face in her hands. She stared into his eyes, her love burning into his like a beacon of hope.

"You already are," she whispered before kissing him.

"I want to be your wife, Gabriel Sloan. Your *real* wife." She slipped from his arms, stepped out of the hot tub and reached out a hand.

As if in a dream, Gabe followed, his fingers threading through hers. She led him through the patio doors and into the room he'd built especially for them.

He stared at her in the darkness, thankful that only the moon cast a glow. Gently, tenderly, he set her away from him.

"This isn't right," he whispered sadly. "It's like before. I'll be taking, and I still can't say what you want to hear. I'm not sure I'll ever be able to do that." He swallowed hard. "I can't love anyone, Blair. That part of me is dead."

She stood there, her swimsuit dark in the moonbeam that flickered through the skylight. Her eyes glistened with unshed tears, unfathomable in the dimness, until she took two steps closer to him.

"It isn't the same, Gabe. Not at all. We're married, and I've committed my life to you. I'm not going to run away, to hide, to wish for more." Her fingers grasped his shirtfront and pulled his face to within inches of hers.

"I love you *exactly* as you are, Gabriel Sloan. Isn't that enough?" She turned away for a moment, and his heart ached as he watched her walk away. When she returned, she held a sheaf of papers in her hand, which she laid on the table in front of him.

"I know you still feel this is necessary. You've kept them hidden, waiting for the right time to ask me to sign them. That's okay. I don't need the security of your money or your company to love you,'' she whispered, turning pages until she came to the final one. Quickly, with a flourish, the prenuptial papers were signed. She folded them and slid them into the envelope, then held them out. ''I love you. I know there are no guarantees with love, but that's okay with me. Love is enough.''

Gabe set the envelope on the table as if it burned his fingers, but he couldn't deny the relief he felt. At Blair's questioning touch, he pulled her into the circle of his arms, closing his eyes as the warmth of her love enfolded him once more.

It was enough for her, but was it enough for him? Would she ever really *need* him the way he needed her in his life?

Would he one day regret not being able to say those words, to give her the love she deserved?

Please, God, show me what love is.

Chapter Twelve

Blair whooshed a breath of air in the stillness of her workroom, the sparkle of her rings shafting a glow of happiness straight to her heart.

"My life might be close to paradise in that castle," she grunted as she heaved a pail of honey out of the way. "But it's pure labor on this side of the tracks."

"Hey, Busy Bee, how's it going?" Mac leaned against the doorway, watching from under the brim of his cap.

"It's going." Blair swiped a hand across her forehead and reached for another frame. "It's only mid-July and so far I've got more honey than in any previous year." She struggled to cut the wax free of the frame. "I wish I could afford a machine to do this. It's so time-consuming."

"Ask and ye shall receive." Mac grinned, stepped to the side and waved a hand. "Tada! Enter, gentlemen."

Albert risked one shy smile before turning his attention to the machine he and Gabe carried inside.

"What's this?" She watched as Gabe plugged it in and Albert demonstrated the machine's ability to uncap the honey in one quick step. "You guys are geniuses!"

Gabe winked at Mac. "I've been telling her that for ages."

"I hope you don't mind that I've been watching you," Albert murmured, his head down. "I had to see exactly what needed doing before I could figure out a design."

Blair laughed in delight as she moved one frame then another through, watching the wax pile neatly. Soon she had enough frames ready to start the extractor.

"Come and watch anytime," she invited. "If this is the result, you guys are welcome at any hour."

"I'd like my thank-you now." Gabe sauntered over and wrapped an arm around her waist, clearly waiting for a kiss of appreciation. She brushed her lips against his cheek. Gradually she was getting used to this new, lighter-hearted Gabe.

"You've got a first-rate crop this year, Busy Bee. And the price is up." Mac grinned, smug delight gleaming in his eyes as he watched Gabe fiddle possessively with her hair. "Looks like I did the right thing when I sold that land, don't you think?"

"Mom!" Daniel raced through the door, his grubby face glowing. He dashed over and wrapped himself around Blair's legs. "Me an' Willie got a surprise for you."

Willie stumbled in the door behind him, gasping for breath, her hand at her throat. "Mercy! I'm about to keel over." Her thin chest heaved. "Haven't run so hard in thirty years."

"I won, though, Willie! I won."

"So you did, boy." Willie collapsed on the chair Mac held out, her narrow face flushed with healthy color.

Blair looked for signs that she was all right, then squatted to smile at Daniel. She shoved the lock of hair from his forehead and brushed at the smudge of dust on his nose. "Willie and I have a surprise," she corrected.

"Do you?" He frowned. "So do we! I'll tell mine first."

"No, I meant it's improper to say me and Willie." Blair sighed at the confusion on his little face. "Go ahead, tell me."

"Can I tell her, Willie? Can I?"

It was clear to Blair that he would tell whether or not he was granted permission, but she kept her lips closed.

"You tell her, Daniel. I have to catch my breath." Willie huffed and puffed in an exaggerated fashion that made Daniel laugh.

"Okay," he agreed. He turned to Blair, hands on his hips, a gleam of barely suppressed joy flickering in his green eyes. "Mr. Bart—" He frowned, glanced at Willie, then started over. "Mr. Bartholemew from the Super Mart said he wants to buy four hundred pounds of honey!" He grinned with delight.

"Four hundred?" Blair looked at Willie for confirmation. "But that's double what he ordered last year!"

Willie nodded, her breathing having slowed fractionally. "He said he's had requests ever since he sold out, and he wants to make sure he doesn't run out this time. He's willing to pay a bit more to guarantee his supply.''

When she named how much more, Blair sagged onto a chair. ''Oh, my!'' She glanced at the two local women Gabe had hired to help out. They grinned, raised thumbs up and kept right on working. ''Four hundred pounds!'' She could hardly believe it.

The telephone's urgent peal broke through the rush of excited voices. Blair hurried to the office.

''Yes, this is Mind Your Own Beeswax. I see. Yes, I think so.'' She listened for a moment, then frowned. ''May I ask how you heard of us? Oh, I see.'' She glanced across the tiny room, searching for and finding Gabe lounging in the doorway. She couldn't help the smile that rose to her lips.

''Yes, that brochure was my husband's creation. If you'll fax me the particulars, I'll get back to you with an estimate. Is that all right?'' Assured that it was, she sat holding the receiver until the recorded message asked her to hang up.

''Is everything all right?'' Gabe frowned at her lack of response. In two strides he was beside her, his hand gently covering hers. ''Blair? What's wrong?''

''Nothing.'' She blinked, seeing anew his beloved face, closely cropped head, large powerful hands. ''I think I've just hit the big time. Some chain of boutiques saw that flyer you helped me design and wants to carry our Christmas candles. They also want me to think about creating a special line just for them.''

He grinned. ''I knew those colors would go over big if you just spread the word. Good for you! You're going to have to hire some more help, you know.''

She gulped. ''I know. But there's no room here.''

''Then we'll add on.'' He winked at her. ''These

are good problems, Blair. Everyone wants these kinds of problems.''

''I guess.'' She let him hug her while her mind whirled with the potential of it all. ''I just thought it would take longer. I'd never have managed it if you hadn't made me see the possibilities.''

He brushed a kiss over her forehead, his hand smoothing her hair. ''It's the very least I could do,'' he murmured, arms linked around her waist. He leaned in close and added, ''For my wife.''

Blair couldn't stop the smile that caught at her lips on hearing those words. They weren't exactly the words she longed to hear, but she wouldn't complain. Gabe had changed so much, a little more wasn't impossible for the Lord, was it?

''Of course your work is selling, dear. I knew it all along. Just took a bit of the right kind of management.'' Willie moved beside Gabe. She beamed at him proudly. ''Didn't take much sense to see that Gabe is the man who helped make those dreams come true. I knew the first time I met him.''

So did I. Blair wanted to agree loudly, but not here in front of everyone. She wanted to tell him herself, in private. Later.

''I guess this means your machine will get a real workout, Albert. Thank you so much for thinking of it.'' She gave him a hug and a kiss on his bald spot. ''Now if I could just get the wax purified and treated a little easier. There is a machine, you know. But it's terribly expensive.'' She fell into thought.

Blair didn't hear anything until Mac's voice cut through the chatter in the room and flew straight to her ear.

''Maybe you should just buy the wax outright.

Spend your time on producing candles, not cleaning beeswax. You could sell your rough stock and buy the finished product. You might even design some colors of your own and commission someone to make them for you.''

He scratched his head, his tanned forehead furrowed. ''Of course, I don't know much about that sort of thing.''

Blair stared at him as the idea took shape. ''On the contrary, Grandpa. You are smarter than you give yourself credit for.'' She raced across the room, flung her arms around his neck and hugged him with delight. ''Smarter than anyone I know.''

She began dreaming of possibilities right there in the workroom. So immersed was she, Willie, Mac, Albert and Daniel had wandered off to get a cool drink at the castle by the time she blinked at the snapping fingers in front of her and saw Gabe's laughing face.

''And you say I get involved!'' He hugged her. ''Something's brewing, isn't it?''

''Yes!'' She hugged him hard. ''I can do this, Gabe! Thanks to you and Albert, Mac, Willie and Daniel, I believe I can really do this.'' She giggled as he swung her around the room, giddy with joy.

If the inane smirks of her employees hadn't shoved reality into her face, Gabe's cell phone pealing its high-pitched call would have. He made a face but let her go and pulled the tiny phone from his pocket.

''Sloan.'' His forehead pleated. ''Hey, Rich! What's up?'' He frowned, his fingers rubbing against Blair's. Suddenly, all motion stopped. His face grew cold and hard. ''He what?''

Blair stood waiting, knowing from the tenseness of

his neck, the rigid straightening of his backbone, that something was terribly wrong.

"I'll be there." He clicked the phone closed and shoved it into his pocket. "I have to go to L.A." The clipped, hard tones brooked no discussion.

Blair took his hand and drew him from the room into the freshness of the summer afternoon air. "What's the matter, Gabe? Please tell me."

He lips turned upward in a smile, but no flicker of joy lit his gorgeous eyes. Cold and hard, they stared straight ahead.

"My father's back. He's buying up Polytech shares and offering my employees bigger and better profits if they will sell their stock to him, or at least back him in a takeover."

"A takeover?" She whispered the words, aghast at the man's temerity. How could he do this to his own son? How could he deliberately sabotage the happiness Gabe had found in this one small area of his life?

"I'll have to leave immediately. Rich has already ordered a local chopper to take me to the airfield. That's how badly he wants me there." His jaw clenched and unclenched.

"I know. It's okay. We'll manage, Gabe. We'll be waiting." She stroked his arm, hoping to infuse her words with assurance and calmness. "Do you need me to come with you?"

His head jerked up, his eyes wide. "You'd do that?"

"Of course. I told you, I love you. If you want my help, for whatever it's worth, you've got it."

He stared at her for a long time before his arms reached out and drew her near. He held her against his chest, his head resting on hers. "Thank you, Blair," he murmured at last, the distant purring of the chopper drawing him from his contemplation. "It will be easier to fight knowing that."

She moved slightly to study his face. "Is that what you want to do?" she asked quietly. "You want to fight him over this?"

The air chilled immediately. His arms dropped away. "You don't think I should fight my own father for a company he's only ever tried to destroy?" He shook his head. "No, I suppose you don't. You couldn't possibly understand."

Blair knew she had to force him to look at what was ahead. Part of their problems had stemmed from his inability to get love from his father. He had to come to terms with that.

She gripped his hands, rubbing her thumbs tenderly over the work-roughened knuckles. "I'm not asking about him," she whispered. "I'm asking what *you* want. Truthfully, honestly. Do you want to fight your father on this?"

"Yes!" The affirmative burst from him in heated vehemence. "I want to show him that I will never again be the sissy, the wimp that he terrified all those years. I want him to know that I can take him on, anytime, and win." He paced back and forth.

"You want to punish him."

His head jerked up, his eyes flashed, and his jaw was clenched in a ruthless line. "Yes."

"Where will that leave you, Gabe?" Blair ignored the wild gusting wind from the chopper blades. She knew time was precious, but so was his spirit. "Will you allow yourself to be crushed by unforgiveness? Because, we both know it's only you who will be hurt. A man like that doesn't understand what he's done.''

One corner of his mouth tipped in a sneer. "Vengeance is mine, says the Lord. Is that what you mean?" He waited for her nod. "Well, this opportunity is heaven-sent. I don't intend to throw it away. Then I'm coming back here, Blair. For good.''

Blair sighed, her soul troubled but her face smiling. "Then go, do what you must. I love you, Gabe. I'll always love you. No matter what." As the pilot raced across the road, she stood on tiptoes and kissed Gabe, trying to express all that lay in her heart. "We'll be here, waiting, Daniel and I. Hurry home.''

He grabbed her and hugged her close, as if afraid he'd never have the chance to do that again. When he set her free, Blair threaded her hand in his and walked with him toward the chopper.

"You'll call me? Every day? Do you need anything?''

He grinned and tapped his forehead. "It's all in here.''

"You'll call me if you need me? Promise?" She waited anxiously for his agreement.

When they were less than fifty feet from the helicopter, Gabe's hands on her forearms forced her to stop.

"Thank you for offering," he said directly into her ear. "But this is something I have to do. I've been waiting for this chance my whole life. I'm going to make him see what he missed." He studied her eyes to be sure she understood. "You need to stay here, take care of our son. Say goodbye to Daniel for me.''

Blair held his gaze, imprinting every detail in her memory. Then she nodded solemnly. "Go with God, my love,'' she murmured as he strode across the grass to the waiting pilot.

Gabe sat tall, silently staring at her, as the craft whirled into the air. She lifted a hand, pressed it to her lips and then held it aloft. Blair told herself he smiled and then mocked her own foolishness as the tears welled and the worry engulfed her.

''Rocks don't smile,'' her conscience reminded her as she plodded to the work shed. ''They don't have feelings.''

She bypassed the building and headed up the hill, tracing the steps she and Gabe had taken such a short time ago. When she got to the top, she collapsed on the grass and stared at the shimmering beauty before her.

Why, God? Why did You take him away, just when I was beginning to believe in happily ever after?

Heaven stayed silent.

Chapter Thirteen

"Mommy?"

"Yes, Daniel?"

"Where is my daddy?"

The same words he'd asked months ago, but oh, the wealth of meaning they contained now.

Blair tucked her son into his captain's bed, then brushed a hand over his disheveled hair. "Your daddy loves you very much, Daniel." Of that much, at least, she was certain.

"Why doesn't he come home?" The little eyelids dropped over sad green eyes, reminding Blair of another wounded child and the vengeance he now sought.

"Daddy will come as soon as he can, sweetheart. He just has to finish his work. He doesn't like being away, but it's very important to him. I think we should pray for him."

Daniel nodded and squeezed his eyes closed. His hands folded reverently. "Me first," he insisted, opening one eye to check for her nod. "Dear God, this is Daniel Sloan. That's my name now, remember, 'cause I gots a daddy, just like the other kids. He's a good daddy, and I love him a lot. Did you see the kite he sended me from the big city? I love kites.''

Blair smiled, but kept silent. This was Daniel's petition. He should offer it in his own way.

"My daddy's been gone an awful long time.'' He pried one eye open. "How long?''

"Eight days,'' Blair told him, suppressing a grin when he shut the eye and continued blithely as if there'd been no pause.

"You prob'ly already know he's been gone that long, and maybe that isn't a long time to you 'cause you made the whole earth and everything in six. But it's a horrible long time to me. I want my daddy back. I want him here, with me. We gotta be a family. My daddy needs a family. He never had none. Amen.''

The abrupt ending caught Blair off guard and she hurriedly composed her own prayer. Though it was shorter than Daniel's, it was just as direct and to the point. She wanted her husband, the man she loved, home.

Daniel added another amen after hers, then wiggled under the coverlet. "I know God'll send him pretty soon.'' He yawned. "I hope I'm not sleeping when Daddy comes home.''

"I'm sure Gabe would wake you up if you were.'' She pressed a kiss to his forehead, her throat tightening as the chubby little arms squeezed her neck in a hug. "Good night, sweetie. Pleasant dreams.''

"Night, Mommy.''

She snapped off the light, leaving only the sailboat night-light burning. As Daniel's soft snores filled the room, she slipped out, pulling the door closed behind her.

Blair was about to head to the hot tub in hopes of easing the cramps in her neck when the phone pealed its summons.

"Gabe! How are you? Is everything all right?" She sank onto the grass next to the rose garden and listened to the weariness in his beloved voice.

"Couldn't be better. Finally got them with their hands in the cookie jar. Legal proceedings, Rich says. That ought to hold off their bid for a while. Stock's up again. Apparently some people wouldn't mind seeing Farnover's takeover."

"Farnover's? You've been refusing them for a while. Is that who's backing your father?" Though she'd learned a few of the details, Blair could only pretend to understand corporate maneuvering.

"Yeah. They always did operate out of the back door." His voice died away. "How are you, Blair? How's Daniel?"

"He's fine. He prayed for you tonight, Gabe. He wants his daddy home." She said it deliberately, hoping he would understand.

"I'm not abandoning him, Blair. I'll be back as soon as I get that shyster off my case permanently." Bitterness, harsh and painful, laced his tone. "He's determined to cow me. To prove he's a better man. Well, I'm not caving. Not anymore."

Blair sighed. More than ever, Gabe was sounding like the man she'd left in L.A.

"Daniel doesn't know corporate America, Gabe. He just knows his daddy isn't there to tickle him or wrestle with or swim with. He misses you."

The silence stretched unbearably.

"I miss him, too. And you. And Mac and Willie and Albert. I miss the simplicity of it. The relaxed pace. Time here runs from one day into the next, and I forget whether I called you yesterday or not. Is that terrible to say?" He sounded worried.

"Of course not." She waited, but when he didn't volunteer any more information, Blair closed her eyes and pictured him alone, tired, full of bitterness and hatred. "Are you all right, Gabe? Are you eating and sleeping?"

"I'm fine."

"I miss you, Gabe. I love you."

"I know."

Tears squeezed out between her lids. She'd wanted so badly to hear the words. She needed to know he loved her, cared about her, wanted to be there with her. Was that asking so much?

His voice, when it finally came, was thin and sad, making her heart clench with pain. "I wish I could hold you, Blair. I wish I could just hold you, right now, right here."

She swallowed. At least he'd admitted that much.

"Do you want me to come?" she whispered.

"No! I don't want you anywhere near him. He's evil. He ruins everything good in my life."

As she waited, Blair silently prayed, begging for the right words to say to show him her love.

"Are you still there?"

"I'm here," she whispered.

"Why did you call my son Daniel?"

The words shocked her for a moment. Then she recalled a newspaper clipping Mac had left for her to read. Daniel—his father's name. Oh, no!

Help me, Lord.

"Blair?"

"When I was in labor, the contractions came very hard and very fast. It was a long labor, and believe me, labor is the right word for it. At one point I was so tired and discouraged that I was ready to agree to their suggestion for cesarean delivery."

"But that's so hard on the mother!" His breathing quickened.

"Mac came in to give Willie a breather. She'd stayed with me all through it, and she needed to relax, so when a quiet period came, in he marched." She smiled, remembering his rigid posture that belied the fear lurking in his eyes. "I told him I didn't think I could do it anymore, and he reminded me that my baby was just like Daniel in the lion's den. The contractions were the lions, and he drew this analogy that if I didn't fight to get my baby out, to give him life, the lions would squeeze the life out of him."

Blair grimaced, not totally sure why she'd told him the tale. "It's a weird kind of analogy, I suppose, but I saw exactly what he was driving at. Some things are worth fighting for. My baby was Daniel to me after that, the whole time I fought to get him into this world. And that's what he stayed."

Gabe said nothing for a long time. Then he whispered, "Thank you." Eventually he regained his voice. "That's what I'm doing," he told her. "I'm driving off the lions so my child will have a future."

Blair squeezed the receiver tightly, then asked the question.

"Are you fighting for justice and truth, Gabe? Or are you merely hoping to exact revenge? It's important to know the difference."

"I have to go." The hardness, the edge—suddenly they were back in his voice.

"Okay. I love you, Gabe. So does Daniel, and all the rest of us. We miss you. Please come back soon."

The click of the line told her he was gone.

Alone and unobserved at last, Blair sat in the semi-darkness and let the tears pour down her cheeks. When Willie sank beside her, she didn't bother to hide them.

"He doesn't need us," she sobbed. "He'll never love us now. He's the same old Gabe, Willie. Business first, last and always. He's enmeshed in trying to remake the little boy whose father hurt him. He can't see that he's got a far better future waiting right here."

Willie hugged her close and dabbed at her tears, but she didn't contradict Blair one iota. Instead, in a hushed voice, she began praying for the man who hurt like a child.

Blair pressed the pedal down hard and headed for the work barn she'd called home for the last four nights. The honey crop was heavier than anything she could have imagined.

Daniel, just home from a camping trip with friends, would not be dissuaded from his opinion that his father's return was imminent. If they'd hoped to take the child's mind off his absent father, it wasn't working. Blair wished she had something that would accomplish that for her. She thought about Gabe constantly, wondered how negotiations were going, how he was dealing with it. Gabe had been gone twelve long days. To Blair, they were like years.

She'd worked late the past two nights and hadn't

been home in time for his calls. Mac relayed the information, of course, but that wasn't the same as talking to Gabe herself. When she'd tried to call back, his cell phone was off. Though his secretary promised, in a polite, distracted voice, to relay her message and the new phone number of the shop, Blair held out little hope of a return call.

As she steered the truck into the yard, she forced herself to face the fear that had been mounting inside her brain for days. Gabe had been sucked back into his old life. The money, the things, they'd become more important. Keeping them from his father took every moment of time and concentration. Hatred seemed to feed his actions.

She'd lost him.

Blair dashed her tears and climbed out of the cab, determined to go on with a facade of strength and composure. Albert, Willie, Mac, Daniel, they still needed her. Perhaps now more than ever. She had to be strong. She had to manage alone.

"Oh, Blair, I'm so glad you're here. Willie wandered down a few minutes ago, and she's determined to help. I can't seem to stop her." The young assistant Gabe had hired grabbed Blair's arm. "Please make her stop. I'm afraid she's going to hurt herself."

Blair followed her into the shed and saw immediately what she meant. Willie stood by the workbench, lifting cases of candles that had been packed earlier. She teetered her way toward them, straining to hold the stack intact.

Blair was about to lift them out of her arms when Willie tripped. Though she was in obvious pain, she took great care to protect the boxes and landed awkwardly on her left hip. The graying skin tone and grimace of tightened lips told Blair everything she needed to know.

"Where did you hurt yourself, Willie?" She knelt by the older woman's side and swallowed the bitter gall of panic. "Can you get up?"

Willie's tightly clenched lips grew white, and she lay back with a moan. "No. It hurts too much. I'm sorry, Blair. I didn't mean to cause problems for you. I just wanted to help."

"I know." Blair took her hand and felt for her pulse. "Don't worry about that now. I'm going to call an ambulance. I don't want to move you in case it's something serious. Just stay still for a moment."

Oh, Lord, she's so special. Please keep her safe.

Blair directed her helpers to bring an old blanket, the only covering she could think of. They tucked it around the thin, frail woman. Then there was nothing to do but wait.

It seemed eons before the ambulance drivers arrived. It didn't take them long to assess the problem.

"Fractured hip, I'd guess," one of them muttered as they lifted Willie into the ambulance. "Woman her age shouldn't be working in a place like this. It's too heavy."

Blair flushed to the roots of her hair but she didn't bother to correct his impression. It was more important to get Willie taken care of.

"You go on ahead," she told them, her mind surging. "I'll need a vehicle. My grandfather will want to come, too. I'll follow you."

At home, Mac and Albert sat beside the pool, watching Daniel play halfheartedly in the shallow end.

"Did you see Willie? Silly woman won't give up

on this fool idea of doing her share, even if it kills her.'' Mac crossed his arms. ''Did you bring her back?''

There was no way to sugarcoat it. Blair took a deep breath. ''She's on her way to the hospital, Grandpa. She fell. The ambulance guys thought she'd probably broken her hip. I'm on my way there now.''

''We're coming with you.'' In a few swift moves, Mac had Daniel out of the pool and was drying him off in a big fluffy towel. ''Grab your clothes quickly, son, and let's get going. Willie needs us.''

Albert trundled along behind when they finally left the castle. His face was pale, his eyes huge behind the horn-rimmed glasses. ''She doesn't like hospitals,'' he muttered to Blair. ''She won't want to stay there.''

Blair patted his hand. ''I know, Albert. We'll just have to pray.'' She'd taken Gabe's keys to the Jeep without even thinking, and they piled inside without a word.

Mac gently explained the situation to Daniel as Blair drove.

''Will Willie be okay? I don't want her to hurt.''

''I don't either, son. I'm sure God will take good care of her.'' Mac tried to reassure the six-year-old, but his words didn't quiet Daniel.

''I need to talk to my daddy,'' he kept repeating. ''He'll make it better. He knows what to do.''

Gabe! Blair hadn't even thought of him. ''We'll phone him as soon as we find out something about Willie. Now just sit quietly and let me drive.''

By the time they reached the hospital, they were all tense with worry. The doctor met them inside. ''She's fractured her hip. The X rays show a clear break. We're going to have her flown to Denver where a surgeon will insert a sort of screw that holds the bone together. She'll be there for a few days, then they'll bring her back. She should be up and walking by then.''

"Thank you, Doctor. Could you let us know when we could see her? It's important for all of us to talk to her before she leaves.''

The doctor nodded, then hurried away. Once he'd gone, Blair caught sight of Mac's gray face. His mouth worked impotently for a few moments. His hand gripped her sleeve.

"I want Willie to have the best care, you know that. But he wants to fly her, Busy Bee! We don't have that kind of money. And we don't have insurance to cover that. How will we manage?''

He wobbled, grabbing Albert's arm for support.

"I'll take care of it.'' Blair led him to a chair in the waiting room and eased him into it. "That's what I do, remember? I take care of things. It will be fine, Grandpa. As long as Willie is all right, we can handle anything.'' She saw him struggle to take a breath and loosened his collar. "Are you all right?''

"I'm fine. It's my sister I'm worried about. We have to think about her.'' He leaned his head against the wall, closed his eyes and began to move his lips.

Blair knew he was praying. She felt the tug on her jeans and squatted in front of Daniel. "What is it, son?''

"Are you gonna call my daddy now?''

She hugged him, then set him free. "Not just yet. I want to see Willie first, talk to her. Then I'll have some news for your dad.''

"We should phone him right now. My daddy

would come home right now if he knew we needed him.'' With a frown at his mother, Daniel turned and walked to the chairs. He plunked himself down beside Mac, threaded his fingers in the older man's and closed his eyes, obviously following his grandfather's example.

"I'll stay with them. You go see the nurse. She's been waiting to talk to you.'' Albert smiled encouragingly, and she hugged him.

"Thank you, Albert. You're a true friend.'' She dealt with the nurse's questions as efficiently as possible, greatly relieved when the doctor came to tell her Willie could see them for a few minutes.

"She's ready for flight so don't hold her up too long. We like to get these things taken care of as quickly as possible.''

Blair nodded, then went to collect the rest of her family. They found Willie comfortably ensconced on a stretcher, though her eyes showed the pain she was in. Still, the same old smile of welcome lifted Blair's weary heart.

"I'm so sorry, Willie. I should never have let you—''

"You couldn't have stopped me. Though I'm sorry to have caused such a fuss. And so much expense! Dear, dear, how will we pay for this?''

Mac lurched forward, his face gray and haggard. "We have God as our father, sister. He owns the cattle on a thousand hills, remember? He'll supply all our needs. We'll manage just fine. You concentrate on getting well.''

Daniel stepped nearer the bed. "I prayed for you, Willie. And my daddy is coming. We'll look after you.''

"Thank you, darling." She ruffled his hair tenderly. "Getting Gabe here is exactly what we need. Good thinking."

Albert contented himself with squeezing her hand, and then Willie was gone.

Blair spared a moment to search for her composure. Then she whirled. "All right now, everyone. Let's—" The words jammed in her throat as Mac wavered on his feet, his hand clenching his left arm. "Grandpa, what's wrong?"

His voice emerged raspy and thin, his legs doubling under him as Albert grabbed his shoulders. "Get a doctor, Busy Bee. I think it's a heart attack."

Chapter Fourteen

Blair paced the length of the waiting room for the hundredth time, begging and pleading with God to save her grandfather's life. She was barely aware of Albert and Daniel returning from the cafeteria until Daniel's hand closed around hers.

"Can we call my daddy now, Mommy?" he begged, his green eyes serious. "Daddy loves Mac and Willie. We're his family. He needs to come home."

Blair sat down and hugged him close. "I know he does, honey. And I did call him. But I couldn't reach him. His secretary says he's not there and he doesn't answer his cell phone." She didn't tell Daniel how much that combination of events worried her. Nor did she speculate on where Gabe could be or what he was doing.

Instead she focused her attention on her son and the loyal friend who'd stood by them through an hour of interminable waiting. "I guess the only thing we can do now is wait. And pray."

"Mrs. Sloan?" The doctor stood behind her, his voice solemn.

"How is he?"

"We won't know that for some time. Right now he's in and out of consciousness. He keeps asking for you. I think it might be best if you came with me. Just you."

She nodded, then turned to explain to Daniel.

Albert smiled. "We'll wait here, Blair. You go ahead."

"Thank you." She followed the doctor down the hall and deep into the caverns of the hospital. Finally they came to a room where bleeps and blips of various machines were monitored on the big console at the nursing station.

"We haven't been able to regulate Mr. Rhodes's heartbeat yet," the doctor explained. "He's on oxygen and hooked up to several monitors. Try to get him to relax. That's the best medicine."

Blair nodded, prepared for the worst as she followed the doctor to her grandfather's bed. Mac looked so frail under the white sheet, his fingers thin and gaunt, bluish where the IV dripped into them.

"Grandpa? I'm here. Please try to relax. You need to get your rest. The doctors are trying to help you. Please hold on. Please, Mac?" Blair carefully lifted his unfettered hand and slipped hers into it.

Mac's eyelids fluttered as if he were rousing himself from a deep sleep. Finally they lifted. Blair breathed a prayer of thanks as she saw recognition in his eyes. His fingers tightened around hers for an instant.

"Call Gabe," he rasped, his face contorting with the effort of speaking, his eyes closing.

"I tried." She hurried to reassure him, anxious to

keep him awake and aware. "I couldn't reach him. He's not in the office."

Mac's fingers loosened, and his chest sank as he heaved a weary, painful breath. "Call Gabe. You need him now." The words died away as he sank into some oblivion that Blair couldn't enter.

"I'm sorry, but you'll have to leave now. He needs to rest. We're trying to stabilize him, but it's an uphill battle." The nurse drew her from the room and closed the door.

Blair stood alone in the hallway. Around her, the hospital bustled with medical efficiency, but she paid it no mind. Grandpa might die! He could leave her at any moment, and she'd be all alone.

She walked in a stupor as reality punched her with the utter hopelessness of it all. Somehow she found herself in the waiting room. Daniel lay asleep on his chair, his little body hunched in a defensive curl. Albert rose and helped her into a chair, his face grave.

"Blair, we need to get hold of Gabe."

"Why does everyone keep saying that?" she half-sobbed, her knuckles against her mouth. "Grandpa just said the same thing."

"Then you have to do it. No matter how much it hurts, no matter what it costs you, you have to tell Gabe that you need him here now." Albert's hands cradled hers. "You've been like a daughter to me, Blair. You've nursed me back to health mentally and physically. You've given me so much. Let me give a little back to you."

She blinked away the tears. "Advice?" she asked tremulously.

"I know it seems silly for me to give advice to anyone." He smiled to show he didn't mind her surprise. "But I believe I've learned a lot from your family. And the one thing you do when things get tough is draw together.''

She nodded.

"Gabe is part of this family, Blair. He deserves the chance to be here, to be part of this. There may be decisions to be made. He can help you with those, or just support you. You need your husband. Your son needs his father. Isn't it time to admit that this is one thing you can't handle on your own? Call him.''

"What if he doesn't come? His business is very important to him, you know." She wiped away the tears and recited all the excuses she'd given herself in the past few hours.

"I believe you're more important to him than anything else in the world. What if you deny him the opportunity to show you that? What if you exclude him from the only family he's ever known, the only love he's ever felt? Mac is as much his as he is yours. Gabe needs to be here.''

Having said his piece, Albert walked to his guarding position beside Daniel, bowed his head and closed his eyes.

Blair closed her eyes also, but not in prayer. Her mind replayed the distant past, a time when she'd been so badly hurt. A time when she'd needed Gabe and he hadn't been there for her.

What if he doesn't come now? What if he puts us on hold until his company is straightened out? What if he doesn't want us anymore?

What if he's waiting to be asked? What if he yearns to be needed, to be wanted? Would you deny him the love you promised him?

The questions raged inside her brain until she could no longer think straight. She glanced at Albert.

"I'm going to the chapel," she whispered, and waited for his nod before she left.

As she passed a bank of phones, the pressure inside built to nearly bursting. *Phone Gabe. Tell him you need him.*

With a prayer for help, she lifted the receiver and dialed.

"I'm sorry, Mrs. Sloan, but he hasn't returned. I'll give him your message as soon as he does."

She dialed his cell phone and got no answer.

Blair leaned her head against the cool, solid metal of the phone mechanism and prayed. "I've tried, Lord. I've tried to call him. He's too busy with his old life."

An idea glimmered in her mind. She scrounged through her handbag until she found the decrepit old address book. Gabe's condo number was there. With shaking hands, she dialed again.

The phone rang several times, but no one picked up. Blair moved the receiver from her ear, ready to hang up, then caught the sound of his beloved voice.

"Leave a message. I'll call you back."

Frantically she searched for the words, the right phrase. But the beep signaled her cue, and there was no more time.

"Gabe, this is Blair." She took a deep breath, squeezed her eyes closed and said the words she had never allowed him to hear. "I need you, Gabe. Please come home."

The machine cut her off. Slowly she replaced the receiver. As she did, Blair felt a deep, cleansing peace surge through her body. She had done the most she could.

"The rest is up to You," she whispered as she pushed open the chapel door and knelt in the back pew. Her eyes caught the tender, loving glance of Jesus as he gazed down at her from a painting.

"Please be with *all* the members of my family and bring us together again. Please bring us home."

Gabe stood on the beach in the twilight, feet bare, jacket tossed carelessly onto the sand.

He'd lost everything.

How could his own father have employed such devious methods? The question drew a bitter smile to his lips. Why was he so surprised?

He stared at the water rushing to shore in big, swelling waves that dashed on the sand in a thousand sparkling droplets. And suddenly he understood Blair's fascination with this place.

The wind spit water on his face, tossed sand against his pants, flipped his perfect tie into wild abandon. For a moment, just one precious moment, he forgot everything but the wonder of the world God had created.

The sky loomed over the sea in an endless swath of darkening blue satin. The beach. He sank to his knees and let a handful of the minuscule grains sift through his fingers. How many grains did it take to make a beach like this? God knew. Jake said He'd even counted the hairs on his head!

Up and down the beach, the stragglers were packing up baskets and chairs and sleepy kids and heading home. Where was home? Gabe's gut twisted with longing for the home he'd known such a short but wonderful time.

How could he go back now, a failure, stripped of everything he'd once flaunted? Okay, not everything, but enough so that he wasn't king of the mountain anymore. He wouldn't even be a player when his father got through with him.

And yet, compared to Blair and Daniel, compared to Willie's soft, loving touch and Mac's sage advice and generous spirit, what did any of that matter? He ached to be there again, to dunk his head in that stupid pool and watch Blair's face light up with admiration. He wanted to hug Daniel tightly, to keep him close and safe, to protect him from the hurt that chewed at his own heart.

He loved them. The knowledge dawned without warning just as the moon slipped from behind a cloud and moved into the clear sky. Love? Was this love, this fierce need to be wanted, to be needed by the most special people in the world? Was it love that made his throat swell with pride when he remembered Blair carelessly signing those stupid papers just so she could prove she wanted more from him than money?

Was it love when it hurt so bad not to be able to hold her, to breathe her light, spicy perfume, to touch that curling mass of vibrantly alive curls?

Yes. Love.

The wonder of it made him weak. He wasn't a misfit, an oddball. He hadn't been tossed on the scrap heap when emotions were handed out. He felt love! He knew that fierce longing to protect the ones who mattered most, and it had a name. Love.

Compared to that, what did the loss of Polytech matter? He wasn't destitute. They could manage very well. Willie and Mac would be well cared for. Albert would have his supplies. Why was Gabe clinging so tightly to a company that he'd clearly outgrown? Why did he refuse to sell out?

"I want to be a father," he whispered, staring at the sky with its twinkling lights. "I want to be a husband. I want the chance to prove I'm worth her love. Can You show me how?''

As clearly as a bell, the solution pinged his brain. *Let go of the company. Get rid of the deadweight of the past. Move on.*

"Yes!" Gabe surged to his feet, snatched up his jacket, shoes and socks and raced across the sand, the wind tearing at his clothes, sucking the very breath from his lungs as he headed home.

He reached the boardwalk, chest searing but heart soaring. In a few quick moves his feet were clad. He hurried toward his expensive car, then stopped. His eyes saw clearly where Gabe had placed his priorities. This wasn't a car for the father of a six-year-old boy. It was fast, it was expensive, but Blair would hate it.

He climbed inside and mentally ticked off "sell car" as he drove toward the condo he'd never thought of as home. "Sell condo," he muttered to himself with a happy grin. He parked and took the elevator, his mind clicking through all the things he no longer wanted or needed.

Inside the apartment, Gabe looked around. "Sell ugly art sculptures," he told himself, wondering why he'd ever purchased the alabaster. He knew why. Someone had told him it would be valuable one day. "I hope that day is now," Gabe grinned as he inspected the rest of his habitat. "Once I get this junk out of the way, I can go back free and clear."

It was only as he returned to the living room that he caught sight of the flashing light on an answering machine he'd long since forgotten he owned. He punched the play button and waited as the machine rewound. A long silence stretched across the tape and he almost shut it off.

"Gabe, this is Blair."

He sucked in his breath, dismay clawing at his brain as he waited for her to blast him.

"I need you. Please come home."

A glow flared inside. It flickered, wavered for an instant and then roared to life.

She *needed* him. *Him!* Nobody had ever needed Gabriel Sloan. He knew right enough that he needed her—he needed her more than life. But organized, self-contained, independent Blair needed him?

Gabe dialed the castle, frowning as the phone rang on and on. No one home. That settled it. He strode into the bedroom. He grabbed a small overnight bag from the closet and tossed in the few clothes he thought he'd need, along with a picture album he'd made all those years ago. Pictures of Blair, the Blair he thought he knew. It was the only thing he wanted from this place. They'd laugh over it years from now. He'd say, "Remember this?" and she'd blush and giggle in that infectious way that drew everyone in on the joke with her.

Gabe shut off the bedroom light, cast one look around the apartment and headed for the door. He didn't care why she needed him. The fact that she did was enough. He intended to be there for her. Always.

A hard, demanding knock on the door erupted a second before he yanked the door open. "Yes?"

Gabe blinked. His father stood in the hallway, his hand still raised.

"Hello, Gabriel."

To his amazement, Gabe felt no flare of anger, no rush of hate, no urge to rant or rave. All he felt was pity. This man knew nothing of what a family should be. For that, Gabe felt only sorrow.

"Hello, Father. I'm sorry, I don't have time to talk. I've got to get home. My wife needs me."

"But the company...the deal?" His father trailed him to the elevator in stunned amazement. "What about that?"

Gabe stepped into the elevator, then motioned his father inside. He punched the floor for the garage, then turned to face his father.

"If the company means so much to you, you can have it. Rich is handling everything from here on in. I built Polytech to prove something."

"To me. I know."

Daniel Sloan nodded. He had that smug, facetious grin that had often made Gabe's fists itch. Now he felt only sadness.

"No, for me. So that I would have something in my life. Something to give me purpose and direction." He stepped out of the elevator when the doors opened, then faced his father as the full import of his decision penetrated. "I don't need the company anymore. I have a gorgeous wife and a life that's more important than anything I ever had here. I'm going back to it, and I'm staying there. You're welcome to take whatever you want. I don't care anymore."

His father grabbed his arm as he unlocked the car. "How can you do this? How can you dump it now, when you've worked for so long? You can't be that much of a..."

"A what? A wimp? A sissy?" Gabe smiled, free at last of the old stigma. "Maybe I am." He tossed his case in the back, then turned to face his father. What he saw was a tired old man who had never figured out what really mattered.

"I have a son, did you know that? He's your grandson. His name is Daniel, too. He's six and he needs me to be with him, to teach him, to raise him with respect and love. You tell me, is Polytech more important than that?''

Daniel Sloan, Sr., stared. ''I have a grandson?'' he whispered, his face pasty white.

Gabe nodded. ''And a daughter-in-law who would make your head spin. As well as some wonderful in-laws who care more about the person than his money or his things. You'd enjoy them. They really live life. They taught me what's important.''

He climbed into the car and started the engine. But he couldn't drive away. Not yet. Forgiveness had been offered, regrets tossed away, hatred expunged. But one thing remained.

Love one another.

Gabe rolled down the window. ''We live in Colorado, Dad. Not too far away. Ask Rich. He'll tell you how to get there. You're welcome anytime.''

His father shook his head but said nothing. He stood, a solitary figure, lost and alone as he puzzled it out. ''Your company, this life you wanted so badly—you'll just let it go without a fight?'' he whispered.

Gabe nodded. ''In a minute,'' he agreed. ''It's worth nothing compared to loving them. Goodbye, Dad.''

Then he headed home.

Chapter Fifteen

Blair glanced at her watch wearily. Seven hours. Surely there must be some news by now. She squeezed her eyes closed and whispered one last prayer as small pudgy fingers curled into hers.

"Daddy will come," Daniel whispered. "He's on his way."

"How do you know that, sweetheart?" Blair couldn't stand to think of the disappointment she'd see contorting those trusting features if her son was wrong.

"I phoned him. He gave me his special number, and I phoned it. Collect. Albert helped me." Daniel glanced proudly at the man by his side before scrounging in his pocket for the business card. Gabe had scribbled his cell phone number on the back.

"Honey, I tried that number a whole bunch of times. Daddy wasn't there." She tried to soften the blow.

"He was when I phoned. And he said not to worry.

He was coming home." Daniel's insistent voice rang loud in the chapel.

"Daddy *is* home."

The low, rumbling tones caught Blair by surprise. She whirled to find herself wrapped in Gabe's strong arms, squeezed against his chest the way she'd only ever dreamed of.

"See! I told you he'd come." Daniel hopped from one foot to the other as he watched them. "I told you."

"You sure did, son. And I'm very proud of you." Gabe reached down and ruffled his son's hair. "Did you and Albert have breakfast yet?"

Daniel shook his head.

Gabe reached into his pocket, then held out a ten-dollar bill. "Well, why don't you treat Albert to a big, hearty breakfast. Then maybe we'll be able to go and see your grandfather. Okay?"

Daniel grinned the widest smile he'd ever managed. "Okay," he agreed. Then his brow furrowed. "Where are you going?"

"I'm going to stay right here and talk to your mom. I've missed her something fierce."

Daniel glanced from his mother to his father, then rolled his eyes. "Prob'ly kissing again," he muttered to Albert.

"Probably." Albert took his hand and led him to the door. Then he stopped, just for a moment, and winked at Blair. "If your mom doesn't mind, why should you?" They disappeared through the doors.

Blair turned to Gabe, anger and frustration vying with tiredness and sheer exhaustion as she glared at him.

"Where have you been, Gabriel? I've been trying to reach you for ages!"

He shrugged, his eyes bright as he slid his arms around her waist and refused to let her go. "I've been correcting a few mistakes," he murmured. "Some old, some new."

"But you took so long!"

He tipped his head and laughed, then glanced around the chapel and winced. "Sorry," he whispered. "But if you'd told me exactly *where* you needed me, it would have been easier."

"Where did you think I'd be?" She stared at him, wondering if he was all right. His eyes were too bright, and he was holding her so tenderly. Not that she minded!

"Denver." He grinned at her uplifted brow. "Daniel," he explained. "He said Willie had broken her *lip* and needed an operation and that the plane took her to Denver. I naturally figured you'd gone along. By the way, she's fine, the operation on her *hip* went well and she's resting very comfortably. I got her some flowers from all of us."

"You saw her?" Blair closed her eyes and breathed a sigh of relief. "Thank you."

"She told me to give you something." Gabe stood silent, his head tilted as he studied her.

"She did? What?" Blair couldn't imagine. Truth to tell, she didn't want to. She was too tired, too glad to see Gabe to even begin puzzling it all out.

"This." He bent and kissed her.

"Oh," she whispered when he finally drew away.

"And one other thing. Her love." He lifted her fingers, tipped her hand and kissed the palm. Then he squeezed her fingers closed around it. His eyes riveted her in their intensity. "Is it all right if I give you my love, too, Blair? Forever. Always."

Blair's mouth dropped open. She couldn't help it.

Shock held her immobilized. But not for long. "You *love* me?" she gasped.

He nodded. "I love you more than I ever knew anyone could love another person. I didn't know anything about love. I was certain I couldn't ever feel that. Today I did. I was standing on the beach and all I could think about was being at home with you. Having all of you near, supporting me, caring for me. And suddenly I understood what love is."

He gripped her shoulders, his stare intense. "I never felt it before, Blair. I should have, but I didn't. I pretended I did, but that's all it was. Pretense. But this time I'm not lying. I know what love is. Will you believe me? Will you trust me with your love?"

"I already did." The tears started then, big fat ones that rolled down her cheeks. "I've always loved you."

He cradled her head against his chest. "I know how hard it was for you, Blair. I know it took a lot of trust to tell me that you needed me. If I'd let you down, if I'd..."

She laid a finger across his lips, her smile tremulous. "God knew," she whispered. "Isn't that enough?"

Then with a boldness born of knowing she was the most precious thing in his world, she wrapped her arms around his neck and snuggled against him. "I'm everlastingly glad you're here," she told him tiredly. "Now we can face Mac's problem together."

He kissed her forehead, delighted to let her rest against him. "Mac's going to be fine," he murmured. "I stopped in there before I came here. He told me where you'd be. He said he knew I'd be back. That I couldn't resist a challenge." Gabe grinned, holding her so he could look into her eyes. "He was right. I couldn't resist the challenge of loving you. Thank God.''

They stood for a long time, content to hold each other until someone came into the chapel. Then they wandered outside and sat on a cold, hard cement bench and watched the sun rise.

"What about the company, Gabe? What happened?"

"I left it all with Rich," he told her softly. "By the time my father's finished, I don't think there will be much left of Polytech. But that doesn't matter." He felt immense relief, and nothing more.

Blair poked him in the ribs. "Why doesn't it matter?" she demanded. "What's changed?"

"I have," he told her simply. "I don't care about Polytech. My life is with you and Daniel and the others. I have enough to start something else, if I want to. We'll manage."

"And your father?"

Gabe knew she was worried about that. A little wiggle of joy threaded its way from his heart to his mouth. "I let go of that, too," he told her. "If my father thinks Polytech will make him happy, he can have it. I've forgiven him for the past. I wish him the best. I even invited him out here, if he wanted to come." He frowned. "Was that okay?"

Blair squeezed his hand hard. "That was very okay," she said.

He brushed the gorgeous curls off her face and studied her. "I love you," he murmured, filled with the amazement of those words.

"I know." She grinned in sheer delight. "Isn't it wonderful? I can hardly wait until we're all at home again."

Gabe held her against his heart, his eyes on the peach-tinted horizon. Home. What a wonderful word.

Four months later, in a little restaurant in town, Blair twined her arms around Gabe's neck, her body moving slowly to the music as she danced with him. Gabe couldn't be happier. Polytech had been saved at the last minute and sold to another contender in a secret move arranged by Rich. Gabe was free to live in their castle, free of his obsession. He had everything right here.

Her closed eyes granted him the freedom to study her beautiful face, and he did. When her finger moved to trace his ear, he smiled just the tiniest bit.

"Gabe?"

"Hmm?"

"I need to talk to you about something."

He grinned. He knew what was coming. "Chemistry?" he guessed, kissing the curve of her jaw in a light caress. "Like what puts those little flashes of light into your hair or makes your eyes shine so?"

She blinked her eyes open, their chocolate depths studying him. "No," she said finally, easing away just a fraction. "Actually it's a different science. Biology."

Gabe squinted at her. "Biology?" Would he ever get the hang of this woman's mind? "Uh, okay. Go ahead."

"It's quite a normal event, actually. Happens to a lot of humans." She was teasing him, her face coy. "You'll see the final product in about seven and a half months."

Gabe jerked to a halt, his mind doing a double take as he digested her words. His eyes searched hers, saw her nod, watched her thousand-watt smile reach her eyes. "A baby?" he whispered. "You're going to have a baby?"

"Actually *we* are. Both of us. You'll be the daddy, I'll be the mommy, and Daniel will be the brother. Those are terms for the biological connection between family members." She chuckled at his glare.

"I know that," he told her grumpily. He pulled her close and kissed her so thoroughly they didn't hear when one song ended and another began. Finally he reached down, his left hand enfolding hers. "Come on."

"Where are we going?"

Gabe thought she looked a little confused but very, very happy. Good. That was the way he intended to keep her.

"We're going home. For once in my life I want to be able to surprise *your* family. I can hardly wait to see their faces when we tell them this," Gabe said as they drove home.

When he pulled into the yard, his spirits plummeted as he noticed a car in the driveway. "Company," he muttered. "Why tonight?"

"Come on, you can tell them all. If they don't already know." She grabbed his hand and urged him on.

"Why would they know?" he demanded, unlocking the front door.

"Because they always know," she whispered, standing on tiptoe to kiss him. "That's the way they are."

"Excuse me."

A cleared voice, a faintly familiar voice drew Gabe from his contemplation of Blair's luminous skin. He found his father watching him, an odd kind of smile twisting his lips.

"Gabriel. You said I was welcome anytime. I figured this was as good a time as any."

Gabe swallowed, felt the snug embrace of Blair in his arms and knew he could afford to be generous. He held out a hand.

"You are welcome. Blair and I were just about to share some news with the family. Can you stay for that?"

Daniel Sloan nodded, his eyes widening at the unexpected invitation.

"Dad, this is my wife, Blair. Blair, this is my father."

He watched as Blair engulfed the stiff, formal man in the traditional Rhodes family hug. Not long ago that had been him standing there, getting the same treatment from Willie. Gabe grinned at the memory.

"Welcome to our family. Let's go to the kitchen." She tossed her jacket on a nearby chair and led the way to the spacious, friendly kitchen. "Ah, you're all in here."

"It's too cold to sit outside," Mac joked, his eyes inquiring.

Gabe grinned, introduced his father and had the satisfaction of seeing Mac's head nod in approval. "Blair and I have something we want to share with you," he began, only to stutter to a stop when Willie yanked open the fridge door and pulled out a huge white cake with pink booties drawn on top. "How did you know?" he demanded.

Willie set the cake down, then wrapped her bony arms around him and hugged for all she was worth. "I always know," she whispered. "It's a gift. Just like this baby."

Gabe hugged her back, wallowing in the love. "That's true."

"She didn't know before I did. I told her a week ago that this family would be growing." Mac's smug smile swept around the room. "A patriarch knows things like that."

Gabe ignored the scoffing laughter as he watched Daniel's head peer around the door frame. "Hi, son. Did we wake you?" He scooped the boy into his arms and pressed a kiss against the tousled hair.

Daniel looped an arm around his dad's neck, his eyes riveted to the cake. "Are we having a party?" he demanded. He caught sight of Gabe's father and straightened. "Who is that?" he whispered.

Gabe held him tightly. "That's your grandfather," he whispered back. "He's my father, and he's come for the celebration."

"What celebration?" The big green eyes so like his own sparkled with excitement.

"Mommy's going to have a baby." Gabe waited for the questions.

"Oh, that." Daniel wiggled his way out of Gabe's arms and walked across the room to study the newest family member. "I knew that already. A sister, maybe. Willie told me." He studied his grandfather for a few minutes, then whirled around to grin at his dad.

"Yep, he's ours," the boy proclaimed. "He's got our eyes and hair." He stuck out his hand in manly fashion. "Welcome to our family. What do I call you?"

The older man glanced nervously around the room, then knelt in front of the boy. "My name is Daniel, too," he murmured, tears pooling at the corners of his red-rimmed eyes. "Could I be part of your family, Daniel? You could call me Grandpa Dan."

"Sure," Daniel agreed, shaking his hand. Then he

reached out and hugged the old man with all his might. "We got lots of room in our family. It's gonna grow and grow. I prayed about it."

"His answered prayers started this whole thing." Blair's arm crept around Gabe's waist, her fingers warm on his cheek as she caressed his face. "We have a son to be proud of."

He hugged her close. He was truly blessed. He'd gone from no family to all family, from hate to love.

What more could he ask for?

"Thank you," Gabe murmured as Mac proposed an apple cider toast and Willie cut the cake. Albert pulled out a chair for the newest member of the family God had reunited. "Thank you very much, Lord."

* * * * *

Dear Reader,

I hope you enjoyed Daniel and his family. He's like the child in all of us, constantly hoping. In this day of the fractured society and problems everywhere, a family is just about the last stronghold of love we have. Sometimes even that's missing and we have to make our own families by loving those God places in our paths.

As you journey on through life, I wish you a wealth of love from those nearest and dearest to you. May I make a request? Will you show some gentle kindness to someone you meet along the way? Just a smile, a touch, a caring glance? Who knows, you may unknowingly be entertaining angels.

God bless.

Lois
Richer

Next month from Steeple Hill's

Love Inspired®

THE PERFECT COUPLE

by

Valerie Hansen

Widow Kara Shepherd and widower
Tyler Corbett can't seem to stop their
meddlesome relatives from playing
matchmaker. When they both agree to a
pretend romance, they believe it's the
answer to all their problems. But soon
Kara finds herself falling for the rugged
rancher for real. Does she dare to hope
that Tyler feels the same?

On sale November 2000

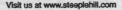 *Love Inspired*®

Visit us at www.steeplehill.com

LITPC

**COMING IN NOVEMBER 2000
FROM STEEPLE HILL**

Three bestselling authors invite you to share in their

HOLIDAY BLESSINGS

by
New York Times bestselling author
DEBBIE MACOMBER
Thanksgiving Prayer
A young woman must decide whether she is willing
to brave the rugged wilderness of Alaska for
the man she loves.

JANE PEART
The Risk of Loving
During the holiday season, two lonely people decide
to risk their hearts and learn to love again.

IRENE HANNON
Home for the Holidays
A troubled widow finds her faith renewed on
Christmas Eve when she falls in love with
a caring man.

HOLIDAY BLESSINGS

Available November 2000 from

Steeple
Hill™

Visit us at www.steeplehill.com   PSHHB